Third
Witch

JACKIE FRENCH

Third Witch

Angus&Robertson
An imprint of HarperCollins*Publishers*

Angus&Robertson

An imprint of HarperCollins*Publishers*, Australia

First published in Australia in 2017
by HarperCollins*Publishers* Australia Pty Limited
ABN 36 009 913 517
harpercollins.com.au

HarperCollins*Publishers*
Level 13, 201 Elizabeth Street, Sydney NSW 2000, Australia
Unit D1, 63 Apollo Drive, Rosedale, Auckland 0632, New Zealand
A 53, Sector 57, Noida, UP, India
1 London Bridge Street, London SE1 9GF, United Kingdom
2 Bloor Street East, 20th floor, Toronto, Ontario M4W 1A8, Canada
195 Broadway, New York NY 10007, USA

National Library of Australia Cataloguing-in-Publication data:

French, Jackie, author.
Third witch / Jackie French.
ISBN: 978 0 7322 9853 1 (paperback)
ISBN: 978 1 4607 0193 5 (ebook)
For children ages 10+
Shakespeare, William, 1564–1616 Macbeth.
Conspiracies—Juvenile fiction.
Betrayal—Juvenile fiction.
Historical fiction.

Cover design by HarperCollins Design Studio
Cover images: Castle by Anxo Silva / Getty Images; Brooch courtesy of
www.alexander-ritchie.co.uk; all other images by shutterstock.com
Author photograph by Kelly Sturgiss
Typeset in Sabon LT Std by HarperCollins Design Studio
Printed and bound in Australia by McPherson's Printing Group
The papers used by HarperCollins in the manufacture of this book are a
natural, recyclable product made from wood grown in sustainable plantation
forests. The fibre source and manufacturing processes meet recognised
international environmental standards, and carry certification.

To Angela,
with true and deepest gratitude,
always

Chapter 1

Morning mist trickled about my ankles. It smelled of cold mud and sweated leather from the men who had trudged across this moor yesterday to fight for King Duncan. I could almost hear the bagpipes' wail as the wind drew clouds across the sun.

Old Agnes hauled up some skinny leaves and glanced at Mam and me. 'Old Man's Bottom,' she informed us.

I choked back a giggle. This was not a day for giggling. Today our thane and men faced the massed swords and daggers of the rebel Thane of Cawdor. Down in the village, women kept their terror from their children while they waited to see if their men came home whole, or missing arms or legs, or not at all. And here on the moor Agnes talked of Old Man's Bottom ...

Agnes glared at me. 'There's naught funny about Old Man's Bottom, girl. The leaves soothe a man outside and in.'

I thought of Lord Murdoch, asking for my ribbon to wear into battle, his armour gleaming on his warhorse. 'Who wants to soothe a man?'

My mistress didn't want to soothe her husband either. She paced and fretted up on the castle battlements, trying to peer over hills and through fog, hoping that after this battle King Duncan would finally give Lord Macbeth the honours he deserved. Which was why I stood here on the moor, shivering. My lady had ordered me to fetch a potion from old Agnes to stiffen Lord Macbeth's sinews and make him ask King Duncan to reward him with the rebel Thane of Cawdor's lands. Lord Macbeth was valiant in battle, but not in asking for his due reward.

'A bit of soothing would do you no harm at all. You'd best keep your head down in times like these,' said Agnes bluntly.

Thunder muttered beyond the hills, as if it had heard her words. The mist blazed blue-white then blinked back to grey.

'King Duncan will win this time,' I said.

Agnes snorted. 'The royal idiot's lost ten battles in ten summers, and half his army in each one. That man's like a kitten that scratches a tom cat then wonders how it came to lose an ear.'

'That was because he kept attacking the whole English army,' I informed her. A village herb woman couldn't know the politics of the land, like we did up at the castle. 'This battle is just against a rebel thane. And this time the king has Lord Macbeth to command his army.' I put up my chin. 'And Lord Macbeth will come marching back again.'

But not with all his men, the mist whispered. *No battle has ever been won with all men left standing*. I shut the thought out.

'What else do we need for my lady's potion?' I demanded.

Agnes raised a shaggy eyebrow at me. When Ma and I first lived with her I'd thought her looks could boil water. But now I met her eyes.

'Annie ...' Mam's voice held a plea.

I sighed. 'Please,' I added.

Old Agnes had taken Mam and me in six years ago, after Da had marched to war and not come home again. Near a third of the village had died that winter, after English raiders burned the crops. Agnes's herb and snail broths had kept us alive. We'd eaten fenny snake and newt soup for a week once, but we had lived. And it had been Agnes's word to a guardsman who'd come to her for a salve for his old scars that had led to me being given a maid's job at the castle when I was twelve years old. The true beginning of my life.

'This?' Agnes held up the bundle of herbs. 'This is dinner for your ma and me. Herb broth boiled up with snails to give strength to old bones. Not all of us dine on venison up at the castle.'

'But you promised me a potion!'

And I'd brought her and Mam a neck of venison just last week. Which I knew she remembered as well as I did.

'That I did not,' said Agnes flatly. 'I promised I'd give your Lord Macbeth enough gumption to become the Thane of Cawdor. You need more than a few leaves to do that.'

'A ... a charm?'

Agnes traded charms in secret, and those who wanted them came to her cottage in darkness. Charms feed the foolish, Agnes said, but what else could an old woman trade who had neither father, son nor husband?

Lord Macbeth was not a fool. 'A charm won't work,' I said firmly. 'Not on a thane.'

'It will if we do it right. The right words, at the right time.'

I shivered. Not at her words, I told myself — I was too old to be shivered just by words. The mist was thickening into rain.

'We?' asked Mam, a quiver in her voice. 'Annie and I know naught of charms.'

'Do you think a thane will take note of one old woman?' said Agnes. 'He'd not even stop his horse to hear me. It must be three who stand across the path this afternoon. Three of us will say the words — I'll need to teach you. A simple man can be fooled by a simple charm, but you need wit and gentlefolks' words to charm a thane.'

'He'll recognise me!' I said, panic rising.

Agnes cackled. 'On the heath, with your cloak about your head? He'll see what we want him to see, like any man.'

Excitement prickled, replacing the panic. Me, who'd once been ragged Annie Grasseyes, charming a great thane! I had no choice, I told myself. It was my duty to do what her ladyship commanded.

'I can speak with gentle wit enough,' I told Agnes. 'But I must ask her ladyship's permission.'

And tell her I would not be back at the castle till after dark. A maid who wandered after dark was reckoned not a maid.

'Good,' said Agnes. 'Bring us back some cold mutton. Not too lean, mind, I likes the fat. And no bannock. It'll get soggy in the rain. Soggy bannock can give you the runs.'

'Make sure your cloak is warm,' Mam told me. 'Wear that nice sealskin her ladyship gave you last Christmas.' She glanced at Agnes and added firmly, 'I can learn whatever's needed.'

Mam was a loyal daughter of the kirk, but she'd take part in a charm for me. Just like she'd gathered nettles till her hands bled to make me broth the summer Da had died. And crouched through the long arc of each autumn day to pick up grains of barley after the harvesters had finished.

'I'm sorry about the rain,' I said. 'You're going to get soaked.'

'Don't you worry about that,' said Agnes. 'Me and your mam are wearing my goose-fat liniment. No one gets congestion of the chest if they're rubbed with that.'

That explained the smell.

She peered at me through the drizzle. 'You'd be better with a good coat of liniment as well.'

'No,' I said, then politely added, 'Thank you.' I could imagine my lady's face if I appeared smelling of old goose and sour leaves.

Lightning spat into the mist, so suddenly I flinched. The thunder cracked like a clash of swords.

'Well,' demanded Agnes, 'when shall we three meet again, in thunder, lightning, or in rain?'

Mam shivered as a gust of rain lashed her face. 'When the hurly-burly's done.' Her voice turned bitter. 'When the battle's lost and won.'

Our thane had won the battle Da had fought in, but Mam had still lost her husband and I my father.

'Just before the set of the sun,' I said. Macbeth and his close companions would surely ride ahead while what was left of his army limped home.

Agnes nodded. 'Where?'

'Upon the heath,' suggested Mam.

The heath was a good choice — though it would take Mam and Agnes six hours to trudge there in the rain. It was close enough to the battleground that Macbeth could return to the king before nightfall to ask for his reward.

'There to meet with Macbeth,' I breathed.

Excitement pounded in me like horse's hooves. If this worked, it would be due to me. And her ladyship would know it.

A cry bit through the fog. Something grey rubbed against Agnes's skirts. She looked down and smiled.

'Paddock calls,' said Mam, smiling too. Cats and dinner were reassuring even on a day of battle.

Paddock yowled her agreement.

'I come, grey cat,' Agnes said.

'She'll have to wait till you've boiled the snails,' I said.

'Paddock can catch herself a mouse. And we have a mouse of our own to catch.' Agnes gazed at me. 'I'll teach you the words now so you can practise. This is the first bit — say it after me: *Fair is foul, and foul is fair: hover through the fog and filthy air.*'

I stared at her. I'd never heard Agnes use words like that before, as good as gentlefolks'.

'Where did you learn that?' I demanded.

'That's my business, nosey nose. Just say the words.'

'Fair is foul, and foul is fair,' I repeated.

'Not like that, girl! Give them words power!'

I thought of my lady waiting at the castle. Of a village girl speaking words that would charm a thane. I let my heart flow into the words.

'Fair is foul, and foul is fair: hover through the fog and filthy air.'

Agnes nodded grudgingly.

I glowed. I'd done it well. They were only words, but I'd felt the air about us quiver.

Chapter 2

Big Rab, the blacksmith, grinned at me as I walked past the forge on my way back to the castle. The flames from his fire shone on his bare arms and leather apron. Up on the hill his mob of sheep flowed white among the heather, tended by Charlie Squint-Eye. He was a fine man, Big Rab, with the smithy and his sheep, a good stone house, and old Maggie Two-Teeth as housekeeper since his ma had died; the best catch for any girl in the village. But I wasn't a village girl now. I nodded and kept walking.

I heard the thud as Rab let his giant hammer fall. Suddenly he was beside me, bareheaded despite the drizzle, grinning down at me.

'A fine day for it, Mistress Annie.'

The thunder snickered. I put my hands on my hips, giving him a glimpse of the silk dress under my cloak.

'A fine day for what, Rab McPherson?'

'For war or love. Your choice.' The grin was wider now.

'A thunderstorm is good for a battle?' I carefully ignored the word 'love'.

'Why yes. The rain will wash the gore away.'

For an instant rage drew a curtain across my eyes. 'Brave men are fighting, Rab, and you make light of it? War is no joke.'

'No, it is no joke.' His face was serious now. 'But that is what the king and thanes make of it, all those fine gentlemen of yours from the castle, riding above the blood and screams in their armour on their great horses.'

'And you make a profit on that armour, but do not march yourself.'

With each battle that Macbeth had fought for the king, Rab had grown richer. None of the castle armourers had his skill. Rab's swords never shattered on a battlefield.

'I'll not be part of great folks' games,' he said. 'But I look after my own.'

I knew that. After Da died and we were starving on nettle broth, Rab had smuggled bannocks to us, till his mam caught him and told his da to give him a beating. A hard woman, Rab's mam, who'd help no one unless they were kin. It was said that when the thane's stallion kicked Rab's father in the head and he died from it, Rab's ma followed him to death herself rather than let anything of hers slip from her fingers. Rab had his father's height and his mother's wits, but his heart was his own.

I let my arms fall. 'It's good to see you, Rab.'

And it was. Most of my good memories of village life had Rab in them.

The grin returned. 'I'll walk you to the castle then.'

'To save me from vagabonds?'

'Nay. The vagabonds will be fighting today, or waiting to steal from the sporrans of the dead. I'll walk you for the pleasure of your company, even though you've a tongue as hot as your hair.'

Lord Murdoch said my red hair was like dancing flames. Lord Murdoch would be safe, surely, up on his warhorse out of reach of the foot soldiers' pikes, and well armoured against arrows. Even if he was captured, his father, Thane of Greymouth, would ransom him. Everyone knew it was better to capture a lord than kill him.

But there was no use expecting courtly words from Rab. 'You'll get wet,' I said to Rab. 'Wetter.'

'I'll dry. And I have another kilt or two, even if I am just a blacksmith and not a knight in armour.'

There must be a way to send away a man who was twice your height and three times the width of your shoulders, but I hadn't found it. And it felt warmer walking next to Rab, even away from the fire at the forge. We were silent for a while. The drizzle thinned. The fog sifted down like flour on the hills, hiding the sheep, though I could still hear their bleats.

'Your ma's looking well,' Rab said.

'She is.'

'She'd be happier at a hearth of her own though, I warrant.'

I shook my head. 'She'll not marry again. There are widows six a farthing these days and no men left for them.'

'I meant at the hearth of her daughter,' he said carefully.

I just as carefully didn't look at him. 'I'll not marry for years yet, if ever. Not after her ladyship's kindness in training me.'

'And what useful things has her ladyship trained you to do? Bake bannocks?'

'I baked the best bannocks in the village at ten years old, Rab McPherson.'

He put up his hand as if to ward off a blow. 'I believe you, Grasseyes!'

Murdoch had said my eyes were the colour of emeralds. Had Rab even seen an emerald?

'I can dress a lady's hair and pin her frock. Do you know it takes a thousand pins just to dress a lady for her dinner?'

'A useful skill indeed. Where would the world be if no one knew how to put in a thousand pins afore dinner?'

'Don't mock me, Rab McPherson. I wear silk now instead of rags. I even have some coins put by. Mam will never starve again, even after Agnes dies.'

'Agnes'll last forever, like the hills. She's been as old as that ever since I've known her. Annie ...'

I thought he was going to try to kiss me in full sight of half the castle. I prepared to stomp on his foot.

But he just said, 'I'd best leave you here, else Cook'll want to know why I haven't patched up her best cauldron.' He grinned. 'I'm mortal afraid of Cook. That ladle of hers could do a man real harm.'

'And why isn't her cauldron mended?'

'Because I have been forging swords for men about to die. Happy pinning, Mistress Annie.'

Murdoch would have bowed to me and winked with his laughing eyes. Rab strode off down the hill without looking back.

I glanced up at the battlements as I walked across the drawbridge towards the castle. There was no sign of her ladyship. The rain must have driven her back to her chambers.

The porter dozed in his cubbyhole as I slipped past. The castle, an old building made of older stones, breathed quiet with a faint scent of mouse. The yells and curses and hammerings of the past few weeks had vanished with the army.

Even though the master was absent, the fire in the Great Hall was lit and the torches in the sconces too. A serving maid curtseyed to me. I glanced at her sharply.

Some of the underservants hadn't taken kindly to a village girl rising so high in our lady's favour. But the maid looked at the floor respectfully.

I climbed the stairs to my lady's chamber, narrow, steep and winding. If ever an enemy forced their way across our drawbridge, two men with strong swords standing on these stairs could hold back an army.

My lady's voice echoed down the stairs. 'Fie upon it! Your tapestry's like an unweeded garden. Things rank and vile possess it merely. Away!'

A door clicked shut. The vast bulk of Mistress Ruth almost collided with me as I entered the corridor.

'I beg pardon, Mistress Annie,' she muttered, wiping away tears.

'Her ladyship is annoyed?' I whispered.

Mistress Ruth flashed me a smile from beneath her red eyes. 'Nothing is right for her today.'

Her tapestry did look like an unweeded garden, but it was unkind to say so. Mistress Ruth had been my lady's nurse. Nurses were not known for their tapestry.

'She's worried,' I said softly.

Mistress Ruth nodded. ''Tis hard for the poor pet to have to wait to see if her husband comes safe home from battle.'

And even harder for her to see him riding home having risked his life and lost his men for no reward.

Instead I said, 'She will love your tapestry by midday, I'm sure of it.'

A steadier smile now. 'You can always coax her, Mistress Annie.'

I smiled back gratefully.

My lady had called me an impudent frog two years ago when I'd told her straight that her arctic fox furs looked like a crone's hair, but that wolfskin lent her complexion the glow of pearls. The next day she had called me to wait upon her. I'd served as one of her ladies ever since. I'd thought Mistress Ruth and Mistress Margaret would resent a villager gaining their mistress's fancy. But they'd welcomed a girl closer to her ladyship's own age, had helped me to learn how to dress and talk and use a finger bowl. ''Tis hard for a young girl like her ladyship, far from home, with just old biddies like us to keep her company,' Mistress Margaret had told me kindly as she stitched one of my lady's old dresses to fit me. And Mistress Ruth had called me 'a good child'.

Would she still think me good if she knew I planned to charm our thane?

My lady frowned as I entered her chamber. Even so she was more beautiful than any girl I knew. Gold glinted in her brown hair. Her eyes were midsummer blue. She had been married but three years, with one babe who had died of the flux six months before.

'Well?' she demanded.

'Well, well, well,' I said, teasing her. And forgetting to curtsey yet again.

She glared at me, and not because I didn't curtsey. 'Do not play with me! I have been sitting, cramped, confined, while you have been dallying on the hillside.' She paced across her chamber. 'Oh, for a muse of fire that could breathe me to the battlefield. I'd teach men how to war, to imitate the action of the tiger, summon up their blood, disguise fair nature with hard-favoured rage.' She strode over to the narrow window and gazed out as if she could see the battle. 'Once more unto the breach, men, once more,' she whispered, 'and choke the battlefield with our enemy Cawdor's dead.'

'Your mother would be proud of your modest stillness and humility,' I told her.

Her mother had been the daughter of a Norse lord and had gone a-Viking with her brothers till her father arranged her marriage with a Scots laird. The laird was dead now, as was his wife, of spotted fever, leaving a son to inherit and marry off his young sister to the Thane of Glamis. A good marriage, even if Lord Macbeth was twice her age, especially now he had command of the king's army. And even better if, with her urging — and Mam's, Agnes's and my help — the Thane of Glamis could become Thane of Cawdor. He would have the largest estate in all Scotland then, except for the king's.

My lady grinned at me reluctantly. 'My mother could go a-Viking and wield a sword, while I must sit garbed in the body of a woman even though I have the heart and courage of a king.' She lowered her voice. 'Where is the potion?'

'I don't have it.' I held up my hand before she could protest. 'Old Agnes says the task is too heavy for a potion.' I went closer and whispered, in case a servant listened at the door. 'It must be done by a charm, at dusk today.'

Would her ladyship be angry? Send me from her service, have Agnes thrown from her cottage? 'Suffer not a witch to live,' they said at kirk. I knew Agnes's charms were only words, but neither the villagers nor the castle folk who crept to her cottage in the shadows believed that.

My lady met my eyes. 'Will a charm work?'

I let out the breath I hadn't known I was holding. I should have known my lady would embrace even charms, if they brought what she desired. 'If there be three of us to make his lordship believe in it. Agnes says Mam and I must be with her.'

'Good. Then you will see it done aright.' She paced again, a wolf caught in a tower. 'What it is to be a wife. Our lives, our souls, our careful accounts, held not in our own hands but in our husband's —'

'I'll need a horse,' I said, stopping her speech mid-flow. Gentlefolk always used a cartload of words instead of one.

'Take Thunder. Tell the steward he needs the exercise.'

I swallowed. I could ride a pony, but my lady's horse had as fierce a temper as she did. But he'd get me to the heath on time — if I were still upon his back.

'Yes, my lady.' I remembered to curtsey this time, but she was too het up to notice.

'What are you waiting for? Go! Make my husband's mind as strong of purpose as his sword! Go and get me Cawdor!'

'Yes, my lady,' I said again.

We met each other's eyes, hers bright blue, excited at the challenge. Then I left.

Chapter 3

Fog sat on the heath like a vast cat on a giant's hearth. Shadows had swallowed the earth, the sky and us. Thunder growled all around. Even the ground vibrated.

I tied Thunder to a bush downhill from the track. A white horse, like the fog. I hoped he wouldn't whinny when he heard Macbeth's horse coming.

My shoulders ached, my hands were blistered and other bits of me needed to be soothed with Old Man's Bottom. Not that I'd ask Agnes for it, I thought as I stumbled through the heather up to the track. There'd be a feast tomorrow. When Lord Murdoch kissed my hand I'd rather smell of roses.

Two figures loomed out of the white belly of the fog. Agnes's hair clung to her face in wet tangles. Mam was no better, pale with cold. She'd had to walk while I rode.

'Did you bring the mutton?' Agnes demanded.

I held out a leather bag. 'A stuffed mutton flap, hardly touched.'

'Spiced? It'll give me wind.' She sniffed at it, grunted, tore off a bit and passed the bag to Mam.

'There's some cold salmon as well,' I told Mam. She found mutton hard to chew.

Agnes was the only woman past twenty in the village who still had all her teeth. When I was small I'd asked if she'd charmed them. She'd grinned and answered, 'Snails. Eating their shells keeps teeth strong.'

'There's pepper in this,' she complained now, delving into the bag for more. 'You should've brought good plain roast venison. Don't know why they bother with this fancy muck.'

I shook my head. 'No one's hunted these past three days.'

'Men are hunting other men instead,' Mam said bitterly, looking up from her salmon.

'Nothing better than a bit of venison if it's well hung.' Agnes gave me a glance. 'Not the only thing that's best well hung neither.'

Had they forgotten why we were out here in the wet? Macbeth could be here soon, my lady waiting all hope and fire back at the castle.

'Lady Macbeth gives us permission to charm her husband,' I said pointedly.

Agnes raised an eyebrow as though she'd had no doubt on that score. But all she said was, 'I'm glad we didn't climb all this way in the damp for nothing then. How much is she paying again?'

'Three sacks of oats.'

Enough to see Mam and Agnes through the winter. Coin is easy to carry, but what use is coin in winter when there's no food for sale in the village to buy with it? Oats could be stored in secret and eaten in secret, with no questions asked.

Agnes swallowed the last of the mutton. 'Any cheese?'

I shook my head. 'But there's quince paste in the saddlebag, wrapped in a bit of leather to keep it dry. I thought you could eat it going home.'

'Can't be doing with quince,' said Agnes, shoving the food sack behind a rock. 'Gives me wind.'

Mam winked at me. She loved sweet things. Every summer Da used to climb the hills to a wild bees' nest only he knew of. The secret died with him. We'd tasted nothing sweet after that till I'd won my lady's favour.

Agnes wiped her chin on her sleeve, then opened a small bag at her waist.

I wrinkled my nose. 'What's that?'

'Soot.' She dabbed some on her finger and reached towards my face.

'I'm not wearing that!'

'So you're happy to have his lordship take one look at you and say, "Why, Mistress Annie, what brings you to the heath?"'

I watched as she applied the soot around Mam's eyes, stroked it below her cheeks then along her neck. I blinked. Suddenly Mam's white face seemed to hover out of the gloom, all eyes and horrid shadows. Even I wouldn't have known her.

'All right, I'll wear it,' I said.

'I'm glad Mistress Annie agrees,' muttered Agnes, applying the soot to me, and then herself. She looked even more terrifying than Mam did.

I felt a shiver of triumph. Yes, this could work.

'You remember what we rehearsed?'

'Of course,' I said impatiently. I'd had to learn a lot more than a few verses in the past four years.

Agnes turned to Mam, her voice suddenly a cackle. 'Where hast thou been, sister?'

I blinked at her. I'd never have recognised her voice. She sounded ... evil.

But this wasn't evil, I told myself. Just play-acting to convince Macbeth to claim the reward that should be his.

'Killing swine,' hissed Mam.

I had never guessed she could sound so sinister. She glanced at me as if to say, I do this for you.

Agnes glared at me, waiting for my line.

'Sister, where thou?' I asked, trying to make my voice as harsh as a crow's.

Agnes settled into the speech. 'A sailor's wife had chestnuts in her lap, and munched, and munched, and munched ...'

Just words, I told myself. And yet, spoken in the fog, from her black-shadowed face, they chilled me.

'"Give me," quoth I.' Agnes's voice was a frog's croaking from the marsh. '"Aroint thee, witch!" the rump-fed ronyon cries. Her husband's to Aleppo gone, master of the Tiger: But in a sieve I'll thither sail, and, like a rat without a tail, I'll do, I'll do, and I'll do.'

'I'll give thee a wind,' hissed Mam obediently.

'Thou art kind,' said Agnes.

'And I another,' I added, still attempting to be a crow.

'I myself have all the other,' declared Agnes's croak. 'I will drain him dry as hay! Though his ship cannot be lost, yet it shall be tempest-tossed.'

I blinked. Suddenly I could see him, a poor man lost far from home, pining, dying, never knowing why ... No! This was play-acting. Only words. And yet ...

'Look what I have,' crowed Agnes.

'Show me!' hissed the voice that wasn't Mam.

'Here I have a pilot's thumb, wrecked as homeward he did come ...'

The thunder snickered, as if it knew a joke we couldn't share. No, that wasn't thunder. Those were hooves!

'A drum, a drum!' I said urgently. 'Macbeth has come.'

Agnes held out her hands to us. Hers was warm, despite the fog. Mam's was cold, like mine.

We circled across the road, chanting: 'The weird sisters, hand in hand, posters of the sea and land, thus do go about, about: thrice to thine, and thrice to mine, and thrice again to make up nine.'

'Peace,' muttered Agnes. 'The charm's wound up.'

A man's voice said, 'So foul and fair a day I have not seen.'

We turned, our blackened faces shimmering in the fog and gloom, and there they were, letting their tired horses walk for a stretch. Two men: Lord Macbeth and his friend Lord Banquo. Both looked weary, but I could see by their faces that this time, finally, the king had won.

Yes, I thought, the king owes Macbeth for this.

Macbeth saw us first. He pulled at his reins, startled.

'How far —' began Lord Banquo, then stopped too. 'What are these,' he muttered to Macbeth, 'so withered and so wild in their attire, that look not like the inhabitants of the earth and yet are on it? Live you?' he demanded, staring at Agnes and trying not to show his fear. 'Or are you aught that man may question?'

Even after a battle, I thought, gentlefolk will still spout a speech.

Agnes nudged me, then put her bristly finger on her lips. Mam and I copied her.

Banquo gazed at us as if we had thrust our tombstones aside and risen from the grave.

'You seem to understand me,' he whispered. 'You should be women, and yet your beards forbid me to interpret that you are so.'

It's only soot and fog, I thought. And yet despite the cold I seemed to burn, as if these minutes were the most important in my life. Two great lords trembled in front of me. I would charm the Thane of Glamis! Give my lady all that she desired!

'Speak, if you can,' demanded Macbeth. 'What are you?'

Agnes stepped forward. 'All hail, Macbeth,' she cried, as imperious as my lady could ever be. 'Hail to thee, Thane of Glamis.'

Mam spoke from the shadows. 'All hail, Macbeth, hail to thee, Thane of Cawdor.'

Macbeth's face was paler than the fog. He believed us. Two strong knights, scared by three women and some words. I felt like I had drunk a pint of heavy winter ale.

I was supposed to say, 'Ask Cawdor of the king and he will grant it ye.' But my lady didn't just want a husband who was the Thane of Cawdor. She wanted one with fire and ambition.

The words seemed to seep into me from the fog. I stepped forward. 'All hail, Macbeth! Thou shalt be king hereafter!' I saw Agnes's startled glance.

The air quivered, as if we hung between the earth and the sky. Macbeth started, and his horse shied in fright. He patted its neck to steady it.

I could feel Mam staring at me. Could feel Agnes *not* staring at me. And yet the words had felt so right. Ripples flowed from me; a stone thrown into a pool.

Lord Banquo was trying, impossibly, to make his horse back away without turning his back on us. 'In the name of truth, are ye fantastical, or that indeed which outwardly ye show?' he muttered. 'My noble partner you greet with present grace and great prediction. To me you speak not.'

He took a deep breath, in control of his horse and himself again. 'If you can look into the seeds of time and say which grain will grow and which will not, speak then to me, who neither begs nor fears your favours nor your hate.'

I glanced at Agnes, wondering what she'd do. She hadn't prepared a speech for Banquo. We hadn't even known he'd be here.

'Hail!' she said, to gain time.

'Hail!' repeated Mam.

'Hail!' I said, because I had run out of ideas too.

But Agnes hadn't.

'Lesser than Macbeth, and greater,' she growled.

'Not so happy, yet happier,' cawed Mam, taking her cue.

And now words came to me too. 'Thou shalt get kings though thou be none. So all hail, Macbeth and Banquo!'

'Banquo and Macbeth, all hail!' Agnes called hurriedly. She grabbed my hand and tugged me off the path into the fog.

Mam followed.

'Stay, you imperfect speakers!' yelled Macbeth. 'Tell me more. By Sinel's death I know I am Thane of Glamis; but how of Cawdor? The Thane of Cawdor lives.'

His horse stepped off the path into the fog a dozen steps, before he pulled at the reins. The ground was treacherous with bog and well he knew it.

'Say from whence you owe this strange intelligence?' he called after us. 'Speak, I charge you.'

Agnes stuck her fingernails into my palm, warning me not to answer. We stood still as the fog swirled about us. Moisture dripped down our faces. Mam's and Agnes's were streaked with black. I supposed mine was too.

'The earth hath bubbles, as the water has, and these are of them,' said Banquo at last, almost succeeding in not sounding terrified. 'Whither are they vanished?'

'Into the air,' said Macbeth unsteadily. 'And what seemed corporal melted as breath into the wind. Would they had stayed.'

'Were such things here as we do speak about?' whispered Banquo. 'Or have we eaten on the insane root that takes the reason prisoner?'

I moved closer, soft-footed through the heather. I could just make out Macbeth's face staring at Banquo.

'Your children shall be kings,' he said quietly.

'*You* shall be king,' Banquo replied.

They believed us!

'And Thane of Cawdor too. Went it not so?' Macbeth sounded breathless.

'To the selfsame tune and words.'

We heard more hoof beats. Agnes clutched me. We stepped back carefully so as not to trip.

'Who's here?' cried Banquo as riders loomed out of the fog. 'Lord Ross!'

'Great tidings,' called the rider. 'The king hath happily received, Macbeth, the news of thy success. Every one did bear thy praises in his kingdom's great defence! And so he bade me, from him, call thee Thane of Cawdor. Hail, most worthy thane! For it is thine.'

And that was how Lord Macbeth became the Thane of Cawdor, just as my lady had demanded, and Mam and Agnes and I watched, the soot dripping off us, as he and his men galloped back into the night towards the king.

Chapter 4

'Why did you say all that stuff about kings?' hissed Agnes, still grasping my hand.

I pulled away. 'My lady wanted a husband with fire and ambition, not just Cawdor. Macbeth *is* Thane of Cawdor now.'

'And always would have been,' said Agnes flatly. 'Else I'd not have done the charm.'

I stared at her. Her face looked dreadful, all striped in black and white. She pulled out a rag tucked into her petticoats and began to wipe the mess away.

'You only ever make a charm for what you know will happen,' she muttered angrily. 'A shy man wants a love charm, but you don't give it unless the lass glances his way first. A soldier wants a charm to keep him safe in battle.' She shrugged. 'You give it to him knowing that if he lives he'll think it worked, and if he doesn't he's beyond complaint. But this!'

'It was only words.'

'Words have power, you stupid child.'

'They don't!'

'They do,' said Mam softly. She took Agnes's rag and began to wipe my face as if I was a baby. I let her. She'd do it better than I, and I must be clean before I went back to the castle. 'Your father said "I love you" and the world turned green and bright.'

'That's different.'

'You'll learn,' said Mam. 'The first time your baby calls you "Mam". That's a flower opening that never fades. Or words of forgiveness on a death bed.' She looked at Agnes. 'Or a friend saying, there's soup for you and your child at my hearth as long as you may need it. Words can change a life, can make or take it.'

I turned to Agnes. 'How did you know the king would make Macbeth Thane of Cawdor today?' Agnes just grinned at me, showing her strong teeth. 'From the soldiers who came to you for charms?' I said slowly.

'Of course,' she said. 'Macbeth's men have been gossiping more than village women at the well. Who else would get Cawdor except the leader of the army that defeated him?'

'Then my lady worried for nothing?'

Agnes shrugged. 'What does she know of the world, except for halls and castles? No harm done to make her grateful to you, and oats for me and your mam. But now!' She shook her head. 'Now you have gone and promised those two men far more than fate should bring. A kingdom for one; sons who will be kings for the other.'

'What can it matter?' I argued. 'It's like the charm for soldiers. Macbeth will spend his life in hope and ambition, and when he dies his last words won't be, "I'm not king yet. The old hag on the heath lied." And the promise to Lord Banquo was for long after his lifetime.'

Agnes stared at me. Even with her face (mostly) clean, she looked different up here in the mist, not the grumbling old lady who'd share her last bannock — or Old Man's Bottom. She looked ... different. 'What you whispered here tonight may grow into a wind from hell.'

'No,' I said stubbornly. 'Lord Macbeth has Cawdor's land and titles, just as my lady wished. And he'll watch out for his own advancement now, as my lady wished.'

Suddenly Agnes seemed to dwindle in the growing dark, an old woman, wet and weary. 'Perhaps,' she said. 'I am for my bed, and a long way it is to trudge to it.'

I glanced at Mam. She was drooping too. 'Can you ride with me?' I asked them.

I knew both Agnes and Mam could ride the shaggy Highland ponies. And with three on his back, my lady's horse should be quieter than with just me.

Agnes looked down at Thunder consideringly as he nosed the wet grass. 'Never met a horse I couldn't humble.'

'Another charm?' I asked, still smarting from her rebuke.

'A good biff across the nose. He knows I'll give it to him. A horse is but a pony that thinks himself above the rest.' Thunder looked up at us. He shuffled his hooves, almost as if embarrassed. Agnes turned her sharp eyes on me. 'When your lady hears the news, tell her to send me a good fatty sheep's pluck.'

I wouldn't tell my lady any such thing. But Cook would give me the meat if I said it was for Mam.

Agnes was already hobbling down the hill. 'Come on, girl!' she called. 'You'll have to give me a leg up.'

The mist turned to rain again, and the rain to knives of ice. Thunder ambled along, subdued by the extra weight on his back, or the rain, or Agnes's bony knees digging into his sides. I had never felt so cold. But at least Mam seemed warm between me and Agnes.

At last we saw the village down in the glen. I stopped the horse by Agnes's cottage.

'Mrrew?' Paddock glared at us on the doorstep, hungry, wet, and it was all our fault.

A thin straggle of smoke wriggled from the chimney. Agnes had the knack of laying a peat fire that would burn all night and half the day. She and Mam would soon be warm and full of broth. I wished I could go inside with them, sleep warm by the hearth on old sheepskins. It seemed a long cold way to the castle. But that was where my lady waited, and my life ...

I fumbled with the bag of food, my hands numb, and passed it down to Mam. 'Here. I'll bet Paddock won't turn her nose up at stuffed mutton.'

'Her?' Agnes snorted. 'She's probably crunched down a nice fat bat. She just likes people waiting on her.' She gave me a look that could cut a stone in two. 'Like that lady of yours. Watch your step now. It's not good to have fine folks notice you too much, in times like these. Just say "yes, my lady" and empty her chamber pot, and then stay out of sight.'

'All right,' I said wearily. I felt … strange. As if the world hung crooked.

Her eyes could have broken ice too. 'And you're not intending to do any such thing, are you?'

And waste all that we'd achieved today? My mistress grateful to me, and Lady of Cawdor now.

Agnes gazed at me. 'Listen to me, girl! When men have the blood of war coursing through their bodies, a breeze can blow a feather, a feather can knock a crumb to the floor, a mouse can take the crumb, a cat can take the mouse and push over a cauldron, the cauldron's fat spills into the fire, and the fire takes a castle.'

'Just be careful, Annie,' whispered Mam.

'Of course I will,' I said wearily. I wanted a few hours' sleep, not a lecture. 'Good night,' I added quickly, and urged the horse for home.

He was eager now, sensing his oats; I didn't even have to guide him. I shut my eyes, half dozing. And when I opened them, the rain had lifted and the stars shone like red daggers above Glamis.

I woke the porter, who woke the groom, who took my lady's horse. The castle staff must have decided their thane would not be back tonight. Only one narrow window in the castle glowed: the red firelight in my lady's chamber. I stumbled up the stairs, more tired than I'd ever been, and scratched on her door.

She opened it herself, dressed for bed, her hair plaited. Her eyes could have cleaved me like a sword. I slipped inside, breathing the warm air, the scent of roses. My lady shut the door behind me. 'Well?' she demanded.

'It's done,' I whispered.

Her body uncoiled slightly. 'The battle won? He was convinced? Sped like an arrow back to the king to ask for his reward?'

'Yes. No.' My tongue was thick with tiredness, my brain like bannock dough. I longed to sit by the fire, to lift my dress to warm my legs. But you couldn't do that in the presence of a lady. 'Lord Macbeth won the battle for the king. We met him on the track with Lord Banquo.'

'And then?' she demanded.

Should I tell her I'd promised Macbeth more than

Cawdor? *Keep your head down*, Agnes had said. Besides, it was no matter. Only words.

'We said the charm. And then a messenger came from the king. Cawdor is yours. Lord Macbeth rode back to thank the king. He will not return here tonight.'

'What?' My lady glowed, bright as the firelight. 'Well may Duncan thank my husband. A dog shows greater gratitude than our king. How did my lord seem?' she added eagerly. 'Humble? Or did you fire him with ambition too?'

'I ... I think so. Yes, I did,' I added more firmly, remembering the look on Lord Macbeth's face when I'd promised he would be king. I tried to find the right words. 'He feels the kiss of ambition now.'

'At last,' she said softly. 'A good day's work, for both of us.'

I wondered if she meant herself and me and the supposed charm; or did she mean herself and Macbeth? He had won one battle; she another. I should have felt triumphant. Instead I just wanted to strip off my wet clothes — even sealskin didn't keep out so many hours of rain — and sleep.

My lady strode to the window and gazed at the red gleam of stars. 'So,' she murmured. 'What next?'

'I do not understand, my lady,' I said wearily.

She turned, her expression impossible to read. 'A high position is but a platform to leap to one much greater.'

'But, my lady, Cawdor is the highest thaneship in the land. No other man has half the estate that Lord Macbeth does now, except the king.'

'Except the king,' she repeated softly. She looked out at the sharp-edged stars again. 'Well, we shall see. Our estate is what we make it.'

'Yes, my lady,' I said obediently.

But she was wrong. A lady could choose to be a wife, or to take the veil, or to go on pilgrimage to Rome, or ... My mind came to the edge of a cliff. I did not know what other choices nobility might make. A village girl had no choice but to obey her superiors. And yet I hadn't obeyed this afternoon. Or had I?

My lady smiled suddenly, as if her thoughts had returned to me and this room. 'To bed,' she said briskly. 'You must be frozen. No doubt my lord will send word of the battle and his new estate tomorrow.' She eyed me sharply. 'You will not speak of this.'

'Of course not, my lady.'

To talk of charms would hurt me far more than it would damage her. And Mam, and Agnes. But we had got my lady her prize of Cawdor. No, my weary mind corrected me: Cawdor had already been given before we even set out. What *had* I done today ...?

'Take the truckle bed.' She nodded to the small bed next to her own.

'Thank you, my lady,' I said gratefully. Her room was

the warmest in the castle. My toes felt lost in ice. I waited for her to go to bed, so I could too. But she looked at me, assessing.

'I must think how to reward you. How does Murdoch of Greymouth suit you?'

I blinked at the change in subject. 'Most well, my lady. A courteous and handsome man.'

'And his family is loyally pledged to ours. Well, we shall see.'

What did she mean? I was too tired to think.

I held the bedclothes back for her to slip between them, then went into the small room next door where a ewer of water and a basin waited for my lady in the morning. Well, Mistress Margaret would have to call for more. I washed quickly, leaving my filthy clothes in a puddle on the floor for the maids. The clean shift felt soft on my cold skin.

I opened my lady's door and crept back into the welcome heat of the apple-wood fire and rose-scented sheets. I said my prayers under my breath, so as not to disturb my lady. But tonight, of all nights, I needed to say them. Only words, but words had power, Mam said. She'd be asleep by Agnes's fire ...

Then I slept too.

Chapter 5

Lord Macbeth's messenger finally galloped across the drawbridge mid-morning. The sun shone with all the heat it had failed to give us, or the men in battle, the day before.

My lady had given out that as Macbeth must surely have defeated the rebels, we must welcome him appropriately. The courtyard was already afloat with chicken feathers and goose down, and peacock blood stained the paving stones. The protesting bleats of sheep ended abruptly as their throats were cut. The porter had hobbled down to the village at dawn to tell any boy old enough to poach his lordship's woods and rivers that there'd be a reward and no questions asked for salmon, trout, pheasant or hare.

I heard the messenger's hoof beats as I pinned on the last sleeve of her ladyship's dress. I glanced at her for permission, then ran to the window and leaned across its deep stone sill.

'The messenger wears the plaid of Glamis, your ladyship.'

'Is his cockade black, white or red?' Black for the death of the laird; white for loss of the battle; red if Macbeth had won.

The other ladies took her calmness for self-control. It was strange to think that in this whole castle, only my ladyship and I knew Macbeth was not just safe but had also been made Thane of Cawdor. And what of Lord Murdoch? Was he safe as well?

'Red, my lady.'

She smiled, and gave Mistress Margaret her hand to slip on her rings. 'Of course he has won! I would have as soon doubted that the sun will rise than his lordship face defeat in battle.' She turned to Mistress Ruth. 'If it is a message, bring the man here. If it is a letter, that itself will do.'

I took the comb and ran it through her hair as she sat upon a cushion. Soon Mistress Ruth was panting back into the chamber — the stairs tried her stoutness.

'A letter, my lady.'

Lady Macbeth stood. She gave the letter one quick glance, her face lighting as tinder does to the spark. 'He is safe. And not just victorious, but made Thane of Cawdor too!'

Mistress Margaret clapped her hands. I tried to look surprised.

'Oh, lambkin, to see you made Lady of Cawdor,' cried Mistress Ruth, then flushed. 'I mean, your ladyship.'

My lady smiled. ''Tis well we planned to feast today! Mistress Ruth, tell the steward to see to the cellars. We must have wine as well as ale. Mistress Margaret, we need a fitting conclusion for our feast. A marzipan centrepiece of Scotland perhaps, with the colours of Glamis, Cawdor and the king.'

Mistress Margaret curtseyed. 'Yes, my lady.'

Mistress Margaret was the daughter of a minor thane, but had never had beauty nor dowry enough for anyone to court her. She had helped to manage my lady's mother's household and there was none to equal her in fashioning a feast to look as grand as its ingredients. I hid my grin. My lady couldn't have found better tasks to keep both women occupied. It would take hours to create a centrepiece so grand, nor would Mistress Ruth be soon up from her discussion in the cellars. They curtseyed and hurried out.

My lady's smile faded as she bent to the letter again. I held my breath. Had Lord Macbeth told her what I'd said about being king one day? Her face said nothing.

'My lady,' I said hesitantly. 'Does his lordship say how the other lords fared in battle? Lord Murdoch?'

She shook her head. 'He does not mention them,' she said absently. 'Surely he would have, if any had been hurt, or captured for ransom.' She put the parchment down and looked at me. 'So, my husband is now Thane of Cawdor as well as Glamis. Yet do I fear his nature; it is too full of the milk of human kindness to catch the nearest way. He would be great; he is not without ambition, but without the illness should attend it.'

'What illness is that, my lady?'

'That sickness which cries, "Thus thou must do, if thou have it!"' She crossed to her window. I remembered Agnes's words. My lady's world was indeed this castle, despite her rides on Thunder. This window was her only daily glimpse of the world beyond. 'Hie thee hither, husband,' she whispered, 'that I may pour my spirits in thine ear; and chastise with the valour of my tongue all that impedes thee from the golden round.'

Gentlefolks' speech was still hard for me to understand sometimes. I was still trying to puzzle out what the 'golden round' was when she turned to me. 'Are you loyal?' she demanded.

'You know I am, my lady.'

'And you have proved it. I will dower you,' she added abruptly.

'My lady? I don't understand.'

'A dowry,' she said impatiently. 'To make you worthy of a proper husband. I will grant it from my own dowry. We can well spare it now. It shall be yours on marriage.'

I curtseyed. It will be linen, I thought, a little too worn for castle use, dresses she has tired of, furs, even perhaps a ring or necklace. 'I will wear whatever has touched your ladyship with gladness and gratitude.'

She looked at me, amused. 'I do not mean petticoats and tablecloths. There is a small estate not far from Greymouth called Badger's Keep.'

My mouth hung open like that of a salmon drowning in the air. 'An estate, my lady? For me?'

'A small one.' She smiled again. 'Small indeed compared to Cawdor. But Murdoch has been loyal to my lord. He should be rewarded with a wife well dowered, and her loyalty returned with a gift from us as well.'

I had dreamed that Murdoch might ask me to marry him. I'd dreamed of dancing in a gold gown with the king too. I'd never thought either was really possible. Lord Murdoch liked me, flirted with me. But even if he forgot his duty to his family and asked to marry me, his father would not allow it. The heir of Greymouth couldn't marry a village girl, even one who wore silks and knew how to use a fork to eat her sweetmeats. But if I brought an estate and the favour of the Lady of Cawdor and Glamis? The old man would be dancing a jig if his back wasn't so stiff. Maybe I should bring the Thane of Greymouth some Old Man's Bottom as well as Badger's Keep. I grinned. Murdoch, the handsomest man in the castle and the finest swordsman, full of wit and poetry ... I could have danced around my lady's chamber.

'I ... I do not know what to say, my lady.'

She grinned back at me. Suddenly we were two girls, not maid and lady.

'You say most prettily, "All the gold in Christendom cannot sweeten any gift from your dear hand, my lady." And then you curtsey low.'

This was the second time in two days that I had been given a speech to say. I sank into the curtsey. I would be Lady Greymouth! And Mam would ... My grin faded. I tried, and failed, to see Mam as mother-in-law to the Thane of Greymouth. I put it from my mind. We'd manage. Mam could live in a cottage on my estate perhaps ... My estate! What Rab McPherson would think of that.

I rose from the curtsey to find my lady a lady again and not a girl.

'Well?' she said quietly. 'Are Badger's Keep and Lord Murdoch enough to keep you loyal, come traitors, tide or tempest?'

'I do not need a gift to keep me so. I am loyal unto death.'

She nodded. 'I think you are. And now we have a victory feast to supervise.'

I followed her along the corridor, a chick trailing a swan, darting in front to open the doors for her. We had just reached the staircase when someone panted up the stairs. Not Mistress Ruth. The steward.

My lady stared at him. 'What tidings that you gallop so?'

He bowed. 'My lady, the king comes here tonight.'

She stood quite still, as if a thunderbolt had struck her. The steward stayed down in his bow. I felt embarrassed as his face grew red. At last she gestured for him to rise.

'You are mad to say it,' she snapped, as if her only concern was housekeeping. 'Is your master with him? Surely he would have told us so we might prepare.'

The steward bobbed his head. 'So please you, my lady, it is true. The second messenger was sent as soon as the king announced that he would come. The messenger is almost dead for breath, with scarcely more than would make up his message.'

My lady gave her 'be kind to servants' smile. 'Tend him well. He brings great news.' She turned to me. 'Tell Mistress Margaret that today's feast must be tonight's and end with a grand centrepiece to honour His Majesty and show our loyalty and gratitude. And I must have my scarlet gown.'

'Yes, my lady.' I curtseyed hurriedly and ran for the stairs, my thoughts as scattered as the courtyard filled with chicken feathers.

My lady had promised me a dowry and Lord Murdoch, and now I would see the king! I must wear my blue silk gown. No, my lady would order our dresses. Blue and her scarlet would not match. I had forgotten to ask her what petticoat to bring with the dress. The cream brocade perhaps, and silver sleeves.

I ran back along the corridor to ask her, then stopped as I heard voices in her chamber. Not voices, I realised. Just one: her own.

'The raven himself is hoarse,' she whispered, 'that croaks the fatal entrance of Duncan under my battlements.'

She must have moved towards the window for her words faded. I strained to hear, but then her voice rose.

'Come, you spirits that tend on mortal thoughts, unsex me here, and fill me from the crown to the toe top-full of direst cruelty!'

I should not hear this. No one should. And yet I could not move.

The cry sank almost to a prayer. But what a prayer.

'Make thick my blood; stop up the access and passage to remorse. Come to my woman's breasts, and take my milk for gall, you murdering ministers, wherever in your sightless substances you wait on nature's mischief!'

I glanced along the corridor. It was empty. What did she mean? Inside the chamber her voice continued, still low, thick with determination and with power.

'Come, thick night, and pall thee in the dunnest smoke of hell, that my keen knife see not the wound it makes, nor heaven peep through the blanket of the dark, to cry "Hold, hold!"'

The corridor still held winter's chill. That was what made me shiver, as if each breath had turned to ice. What was this talk of knives and wounds? What did my lady intend?

Nothing, I told myself. They were only words. Words like those she'd said yesterday when she'd talked of building barricades with Cawdor's dead. She'd wished to be a tiger then. Gentlefolk liked to speak in images of spark and fire. This was nothing more.

I forced a smile and knocked at the door.

'Enter!'

For a second the face that stared at me was a hawk's, its beak ready to pluck out the eyes of a lamb. I blinked, and once more she was my lady, her face serene.

Chapter 6

King Duncan sat at the head of the high table, with my lady and Lord Macbeth on either side. Then came his men, and then Macbeth's men — Murdoch tall and triumphant among them — then, below the salt, my lady's women, including me, Annie Grasseyes, sitting at table with the king!

I looked at him curiously, trying not to stare; this man who had spent his army fruitlessly each year for a whole decade, trying to gain a foothold on England's soil, but who never wielded a sword himself. He was small, with shoulders hunched under his ermine. The long slim fingers that held the leg of peacock looked delicate. No wonder he'd needed Lord Macbeth to lead and win the battle against the rebels.

For the first time I wondered if Lord Cawdor had cause to rebel, seeing so many of his men marched from their farms and other services every year to be slaughtered for the king's improbable ambition. Had King Duncan ever thought to walk through his villages and moorlands? Had he seen the empty cottages, the sad widows and hungry children, the sheep untended, because of the men he'd sent to their deaths? What kind of greed did this man have?

And yet tonight he ate little: the leg of peacock dressed with onions at the first course; an apple pastry from the second, though he left the crust; candied coleworts and parsnips from the third. He exclaimed at the feast's final centrepiece with all the rest, praising my lady as the sugar snow slipped off to reveal a great army, King Duncan nobly at its head, raising his sword. Which he had not. But he had ordered the battle, so the victory must be counted as his.

Table after table filled the hall. Every male servant waited here tonight; the castle's servant girls and women sweated at the hearthstones, spits and cauldrons in the kitchen. Outside in the courtyard, yells and laughter from the villages surrounded the sheep turning on spits, the barrels of ale, the barrowloads of bannocks made as fast as the cooks and maids could bake them. The whole village feasted tonight too — at least those families whose men had come home whole. There would be dark hearths and weeping in the village tonight too.

But not here at the castle. Mam would be out there, and Agnes too, no doubt, munching the free meat with her excellent teeth and complaining that the ale was sour.

I glanced up the table towards Lord Murdoch. What would he think if I drew him outside, among the villagers, to meet Mam? I'd learned gentle speech and manners from her ladyship. But Mam hadn't. Murdoch must know I came from humble stock. Yet neither would he want it shouted to the world.

He caught my glance and grinned. He stood and bowed to the high table, then strode to me, took my hand and kissed it, in front of the whole hall. My cheeks burned.

'So pensive, lady?' he asked.

I smiled. 'I'm storing up these memories, as a squirrel gathers nuts, to nibble at them in the winter of my old age.'

He laughed. 'You will be as beautiful as winter, your hair turned to snow instead of shining like a sunrise on a stream.'

I flushed again. 'I ... I am glad you took no hurt yesterday, my lord.'

'I have a charmed life,' he said lightly. 'One horse lost under me, which pains me for he was stout-hearted and rode true. But my other bears no hurt, beyond the blood of rebels on his hooves.'

He drew out a piece of parchment from the pouch at his waist, and flourished it as he bowed again. 'I wrote this for you, lady.'

As I took it, I felt the others at my table stare, waiting for me to read it aloud. The writing was plain brown ink, not garnished with gold or images as I'd seen in my lady's books. I hesitated, making out a word here, half a word there. It would take me half the night to work out what it all said. For a moment I almost panicked. But Mam had not panicked when the snow caved in half of our roof; nor Agnes when a wolf tried to enter her cottage the year of the starvation. She'd bashed its nose with a frying pan and it had gone off whimpering. *Think, girl*, I heard her whispering.

I smiled up at Murdoch. 'I would rather have your words to me spoken not written, engraved on my heart instead of on paper.'

He smiled back, not displeased. This meant all the ladies at this table would hear him recite his poem too. What man did not enjoy the admiration of ladies?

'*My lady's eyes are nothing like the stars,*' he began, his voice as clear as any bard's.

'*Stars shine cold for all, and yet my lady's eyes are flaming green*

Her passion running as a stream, that only I have seen ...'

My cheeks grew even warmer as he kept reciting, and not from the vast fire in the hearth or the crush of people. Such words for me!

Nor had he guessed I could not read. I smiled and blushed as the poem continued, and vowed to practise. I would need to cipher too when I had the keeping of the

Greymouth manor. I imagined my children, who would learn how to read, to manage a great household or wield a sword ... Of course! Mam could be their nurse. A nurse had status. A nurse could eat with me, as Mistress Ruth ate with my lady, though not of course at the high table. Mam would have her own room, and be kept warm and safe as she grew feeble ...

'And now I know is not a dream!

My lady of the emerald eyes does love, and she is mine!' finished Lord Murdoch. Those around us laughed and clapped.

'Mistress Annie?' A servant approached — he must have waited till Murdoch finished the poem. 'A ... a person wishes to have words with you. She is in the porter's room.'

Mam?

I stood and curtseyed to Lord Murdoch. 'My apologies, sir.'

He grabbed my hand and kissed it, then whispered, 'I will excuse you all, if I may kiss thee once again, before this day is done.'

I flushed, not knowing how to answer, but he just smiled. It seemed he didn't mind my innocence. I curtseyed a deeper apology towards my lady, who nodded permission for me to leave, and an even lower curtsey to the king, although I doubted he noticed it, then hurried through the crowded hall.

Outside, the air in the courtyard was almost as warm as in the Great Hall. A great wood fire leaped to the sky, the biggest I had ever seen, splatters from roasting mutton sending sparks dancing. I was glad of its heat for I had not brought my cloak. Over by the ale butts a crowd of men sang about a dragon and a knight — one of those songs where the dragon is female and the knight's sword thrust has double meanings enough to set a drunk to laughing.

I skirted them, then stopped as a warm hand touched my shoulder.

'Come to mingle with the commoners, Mistress Annie?'

Rab McPherson.

'You look beautiful,' he added. 'And not just in your fine dress.'

I flushed, deeper than in the hall. 'Thank you, Rab. You look most fine too.'

He did, standing head and shoulders above the crowd, his cloak and kilt of thick wool evenly weaved, so different from the silks and satins I'd just left.

'If you've come to see your mam, I took her home a little while ago with our Maggie. Nay, don't worry. You know your mother — she does not like noise.'

Nor the tales of battle that would be told by the soldiers who'd returned tonight, I thought. I flushed again, this time with guilt. I should have come out and spoken to her; shown her my pink silk dress, made sure she had a helping of the mutton.

I met Rab's eyes and suddenly knew he had escorted Mam and Agnes here too. It wasn't safe for two women, even older women, to be out alone with men fresh from battle and with ready access to ale.

'Thank you,' I said. 'You are the kindest of friends, Rab McPherson. I'm sorry, but I have duties ...'

He stood back. 'We can't interrupt the duties of the castle, can we? May your dreams tonight be sweet, Mistress Annie.'

'And yours,' I said quickly, and slipped away through the crowd, wondering who could have sent the servant.

I peered into the porter's cubbyhole. Agnes sat on the porter's stool, a tankard of ale in one hand, a bannock piled with meat in the other.

She glared up at me. 'Ain't you the fine one! Where's me bags of oats?'

How had she got the servant to do her bidding? She must have given him a charm sometime, or promised him one, I thought resignedly. Or just glared at him till he obeyed. 'I thought you'd gone home with Mam.'

'Not while there's meat on them mutton bones. And when the meat's gone they'll make a good broth too, with a few herbs and a little oatmeal to thicken it. Mebee I could have a bag of bones when her ladyship remembers to send the oats?'

I sighed. 'It was me who forgot. I'll ask the steward tomorrow.'

That was how life worked at the castle. Her ladyship ordered her women, her women ordered the steward, the steward ordered the groom, who ordered one of the lads to deliver the oats. But Agnes could never understand that.

'Aren't you scared to go back by yourself in the dark with all the soldiers about?' I asked her.

She snorted. 'Darkness is the safest time for an old woman. What man can see a black cloak in a black night? You remember that, girl. Stand still in the darkness with your eyes down and no one will even guess you're there, as long as you don't panic and try to run.' She gave my dress a withering glance. 'And supposing you wear proper colours, not a hussy's red.'

'It's pink,' I said indignantly.

'And what is pink but red that's not had long enough in the dye pot?' She fixed me with black eyes like a hawk's. 'I heard you've been casting cow's eyes at that foreigner, Murdoch.'

'He's not foreign. His father's estate is on the coast.'

'Well, ain't that foreign? Don't you be taken in by pretty satins. It's not satin that makes a man, but the tilt of his kilt. Your mam needs grandbabies. She ain't getting any younger.'

And Agnes had been older than the boulders on the

hillside even when I was small. 'Lord Murdoch is a fine gentleman and great warrior.'

'You've seen what being married to a warrior got your mam.' Agnes crammed the last of the meat into her mouth. 'Don't let them scaggins take them mutton bones. And don't you forget about the oats neither.'

She creaked off and the black night swallowed her. She was right. Within three heartbeats I could not see her at all.

I slept in the small robing room off my lady's chamber that night, and Mistress Margaret and Mistress Ruth in their usual room along the corridor. Tonight, of course, Macbeth would share his wife's chamber.

As always, the women retired from the feast early, leaving the men to their drinking and boasting. We bathed my lady in warm water scented with oil of roses, and draped her in the embroidered shift that had been left warming by the hearth, ready for her husband to join her. I placed two big logs onto the fire to see it through till morning. It still seemed strange to waste good wood this way. I had only ever seen peat fires before I'd come to the castle, except at Rab's forge.

My mattress was soft, filled with down, not feathers. I floated deep in sleep, until voices echoed in my dreams.

'If it were done when 'tis done, then 'twere well it were done quickly.' A man's voice.

And then a woman's. 'Was the hope drunk wherein you dressed yourself? Hath it slept since? Wouldst thou live a coward in thine own esteem, letting "I dare not" wait upon "I would"?'

The man seemed angry. Why wouldn't he be quiet? I thought vaguely in my dream. I wanted to sleep ... 'Prithee, peace: I dare do all that may become a man. Who dares do more is none.'

The lady's reply could have withered barley with its scorn. 'What beast was it, then, that made you break this enterprise to me?' she cried. 'When you durst do it, then you were a man! I would, while our son was smiling in my face, have plucked my nipple from his boneless gums and dashed his brains out, had I so sworn as you have done to this!'

Silence.

For some reason it was the quiet that woke me, not the noise. I opened my eyes and blinked in the darkness, then turned over to sleep again.

'If we should fail?' the man said more quietly.

I knew his voice — Lord Macbeth. This was no dream. I sat up in bed and listened.

'Screw your courage to the sticking-place, and we'll not fail,' declared my lady.

What was she urging her husband to do now? Become the permanent leader of King Duncan's army perhaps? Or even chancellor, which would give him a place at court, and her as well. The Thane of Cawdor could certainly ask for that, and might if pushed hard enough. I might even get to stay in the king's castle, if Lord Macbeth was chancellor.

I'd dance in a golden gown ...

Their voices grew too soft to hear. I snuggled back down and fell into the world of sleep.

Chapter 7

A scream woke me. Something loomed in the window, its wings spread wide. I relaxed back onto my pillow. Just an owl, calling to its mate. I was as jumpy as a mouse tonight.

'Good hunting,' I whispered to the bird. 'Find fat rats about the granary and mice among the hens.'

I heard a voice next door.

I should not listen to whispered words between wife and husband, but what if Macbeth had gone back to his own chamber and my lady wanted me? It sounded like one voice, not two. Perhaps my lady had called, and that was what had woken me, not the owl.

I slid my legs off the mattress and tiptoed to the door. It *was* my lady's voice, but soft, the way she muttered to herself alone.

'Peace!' she whispered. Suddenly there was desperation in her tone. 'It was the owl that shrieked, the fatal bellman, which gives the sternest good night. He is about it. The doors are open, and the surfeited grooms do mock their charge with snores. I have drugged their possets.'

My bare feet froze to the stones. What did she mean?

'Alack, I am afraid they have awaked, and 'tis not done.' Her voice was almost anguished now. 'I laid their daggers ready; he could not miss them. Had he not resembled my father as he slept, I had done it.' I heard her door creak open, and then her voice again. 'My husband!' she cried softly, in relief.

'I have done the deed.' Macbeth's voice was heavy.

What deed? I pressed closer to the door as he continued.

'Did you not hear a noise?'

I had never heard Lord Macbeth sound like this before, as if something in him had died tonight, too heavy for him to bear.

'I heard the owl scream and the crickets cry.' My lady's voice was reassuring now. 'What's done is done! You must not think of this again. It will make us mad.'

'Methought I heard a voice cry, "Sleep no more!"' he muttered.

I kept my ear against the door. I could not help it. What were they talking about?

'"Macbeth does murder sleep,"' my lord whispered, so soft that I wouldn't have heard it from my bed. 'The innocent sleep, sleep that knits up the ravelled sleeve of care.'

'What do you mean?' My lady's voice was sharp.

'Still it cried, "Sleep no more!" to all the house.' My lord still spoke in his dreadful whisper. '"Glamis hath murdered sleep, and therefore Cawdor shall sleep no more; Macbeth shall sleep no more."'

'Who was it that thus cried?' demanded my lady. 'Why, worthy thane, you do unbend your noble strength to think so brain-sickly of things.' I could hear she was trying to sound calm. 'Go get some water and wash this filthy witness from your hand. Why did you bring these daggers from the place?'

He would have to come into the robing room to get water, or call for me. I crept back onto my bed and pulled up the quilt and tried to seem asleep.

But no one called, or came through the door.

I lay still, my eyes closed, trying to breathe steadily. What had they been talking about? Had Macbeth brought bloodied daggers from the battle into my lady's bedchamber? No wonder she was angry. But what did she mean about drugging the grooms' possets?

I heard my lady's door open and then shut again. Lord Macbeth must be going to wash in his own rooms. Slowly I relaxed again.

Only words, I thought as sleep crept over me. My lady probably meant that even the servants had feasted well enough tonight to make them sleep, or maybe that she'd given one of the grooms a posset so he could sleep.

The muttering next door had quietened. A mouse

squeaked behind the tapestries. I heard the owl again, calling to its mate as it hunted. At last I slept too.

The bell woke me. Not the bell for morning prayer, but the harsh clang, clang, clang of the alarm bell. I leaped up and shrugged my dress over my shift. Had the Danes attacked?

I ran into my lady's room, careless of my hair, my bare feet hidden underneath my skirts, forgetting that her husband might be with her. But she was awake, and alone, slipping from her bed as I entered. I curtseyed hurriedly and grabbed a fur cloak to cover her shift, the only thing to hand. Her dresses were down the corridor, by the garderobe.

'My lady, what is it? Is the castle being attacked?'

'We shall soon see. Any attackers shall feel our iron. Iron hearts and iron swords.'

She wrapped the cloak around her while I slid her silk slippers onto her feet. I opened the door for her as Mistress Margaret and Mistress Ruth ran down the corridor towards us.

'What is it?' cried Mistress Ruth, forgetting even to curtsey.

'We shall see,' repeated my lady curtly. We followed her as she swept along the corridor, then paused as a man I hadn't seen before hurried towards us, his doublet embroidered with the king's arms. One of King Duncan's men then, and high in his regard.

My lady recognised him. 'Lord Macduff! Why does such a hideous trumpet call the sleepers of the house? Speak!'

'Oh, gentle lady, 'tis not for you to hear what I can speak.' Lord Macduff sounded like a man who preferred his women quiet and, even better, far away.

My lady tapped her foot.

Lord Macduff shook his head. 'The repetition in a woman's ear would murder as it fell,' he said patronisingly, looking along the corridor for someone worth talking to, presumably wearing kilt or trousers, not a dress.

Ha. He did not know my lady. Nor me, nor Mistress Margaret or Mistress Ruth or Mam or Agnes. Who did he think laid out the dead? Or tended the dying? Or brought children into the world with love and pain? Not men.

My lady fixed him with a glare that would skewer meat to a spit. 'Lord Macduff,' she began, as imperious as if she had been Emperor of Rome for two score years.

Footsteps clattered up the stairs. Lord Banquo.

Lord Macduff turned to him in relief. 'Oh, Banquo! Our royal master's murdered!'

My first thought was that the idiot had blurted it out in front of the ladies anyway.

My second was: The king is dead! That stooped, finicky little man I'd seen at the high table last night. Dead.

My third thought ... I could not think it. *Would* not.

My lady clasped her hands. 'Woe, alas! What, in our house?'

She seemed sincere. *Must* be sincere.

'Too cruel in any house,' said Lord Macduff.

More footsteps thudded the stairs. Lord Macbeth appeared, his bloody sword in hand, followed by Lord Lennox. I stared at the blade, at the bloodstained hand that held it. Surely Lord Macbeth hadn't just killed the king?

Prince Donalbain ran along the corridor from the floor above, followed by Prince Malcolm.

'What is amiss?' Prince Donalbain called.

He had the look of his father, weak-chinned and slight. His younger brother, Malcolm, looked stronger, with the muscular hands of a swordsman.

Lord Macbeth kneeled before the princes. 'You are amiss, yet do not know it: The spring, the head, the fountain of your blood is stopped; the very source of it is stopped.'

'Your royal father is murdered,' said Macduff bluntly, then bowed deep to Prince Donalbain, as if to a king.

Prince Donalbain's mouth fell open.

Prince Donalbain will be our king now, I thought vaguely. I have met two kings ...

Prince Malcolm stared at Macduff, and then at Macbeth and his bloody sword. 'By whom?' he demanded quietly.

'His grooms, we think,' said Sir Lennox. 'Their hands and faces were badged with blood; so were their daggers, which unwiped we found upon their pillows.'

The grooms killed the king, I thought with relief. How could I have suspected anything different?

'Oh, I do repent me of my fury that I did kill them,' Lord Macbeth said softly. He laid his bloody sword at the princes' feet, then kneeled before the princes.

Prince Donalbain stepped back in revulsion. Prince Malcolm stared at the sword again, and then at Macbeth, still kneeling on the flagstones.

'Why did you kill the grooms?' asked Macduff, even more bluntly than before.

I glanced at my lady. Her face was white, but I did not think with shock. No, she was angry at her husband being questioned in such a way, before so many, here in their hall.

'Who can be wise, amazed, temperate and furious, loyal and neutral, in a moment?' replied Macbeth. 'Here lay Duncan, his silver skin laced with his golden blood; and his gashed stabs looked like a breach in nature for ruin's wasteful entrance ...'

My lord continued with his speech — a good one. But it did not ring quite true.

I watched the faces around us. Prince Donalbain looked like he'd been knocked out by a chicken. Banquo seemed grieved and horrified. Mistress Margaret wept, as one should when a king has died. Mistress Ruth gazed at my lady's shift under her cloak, as if concerned that she wasn't dressed warmly enough for tragedy in the corridor.

Prince Malcolm and Macduff exchanged a glance, their faces carefully expressionless. What were they thinking? Of blood and daggers in the night?

The bloody words I'd heard spoken had been a dream. They *must* have been a dream.

My lady stood very still, her eyes wide with horror. Yes, that had to be what she was feeling ...

'There, the murderers,' Macbeth continued, 'steeped in the colours of their trade, their daggers unmannerly breeched with gore. Who could refrain that had a heart to love?'

A flowery speech was all very well, but this was not the time.

My lady thought so too. She caught my eye, then carefully swayed. My arms went up automatically to catch her. She was lighter than a half-bag of oats.

'Help me hence,' she whispered.

'Look to the lady,' said Macduff. No word of apology now for mentioning blood in front of ladies. His face was still as blank as a closed drawbridge.

Whatever I imagined, Macduff suspected too.

And our king was dead.

Chapter 8

My lady ate with Lord Macbeth, privately in her chamber. There would be no feasting today. My lady had ordered food taken up to the princes' chambers too. They would not want to dine in public while grieving for their father.

Mistress Ruth, Mistress Margaret and I sat on cushions in the outer room, eating leftover minced chicken and pies and peacock. The whole castle would be eating leftovers for a week. The peacock had looked so fine when it was carried into the feast, its feathers stuck back into the roasted meat, but today it was tough and greasy. For a moment I longed for Agnes's cottage. She and Mam would be eating mutton broth, bright with herbs and hot from the pan, not carried across the castle courtyard from the kitchens.

A thousand suspicions were muttered around the castle today.

And in this room.

'How could servants do such a wicked thing?' asked Mistress Ruth. She wiped her fingers on her napkin before taking a piece of bread and loading it with chicken. White risen bread, for my lady would have no bannock. 'To murder such a gentle lord as was our king.'

'Perhaps the king meant to dismiss them,' said Mistress Margaret, taking a piece of goose and raisin pie.

'But why go back to bed, and leave their bloody daggers on their pillows?' demanded Mistress Ruth.

I glanced up from my bread and peacock. She had put her finger on the itch. Mistress Ruth was no fool, for all she fussed. The grooms must have known they'd be discovered with the bloody daggers. But if their possets had been drugged, they might have killed the king, then sleep had overtaken them before they could hide their daggers. My lady had talked of drugged possets last night ...

'Witchcraft,' said Mistress Margaret. 'It's the only answer.' She lowered her voice. 'It's said our lord and Banquo met three witches on the heath as they rode back from battle.'

I forced myself to chew the peacock. Rumours flew around the castle faster than bats. Banquo must have told a groom, or his servants.

'I don't believe in witchcraft,' I said firmly.

'Nor I,' said Mistress Ruth.

Did she carefully not look at me? She must know I had lived with Agnes before coming to the castle. Perhaps it had been she who'd told my lady that I could ask Agnes for the charm? I shook my head. I needed peace to piece together all my thoughts. But there was no peace here.

Her ladyship rang her bell.

Mistress Margaret answered, then came out with their tray to take to the kitchen. She was back in less time than it took a cock to crow. She paused by the door dramatically. 'You'll never guess what's happened now!'

'What?' I asked wearily.

How many nights had I lost sleep? The wind down the chimney whispered: *Macbeth has murdered sleep …*

'Another murder?' cried Mistress Ruth. I could see she thought this more exciting than stitching tapestry or pinning on sleeves.

'No. Worse!'

'What could be worse?' demanded Mistress Ruth.

'My lord has just had word. The king's sons have fled!'

'Fled? You mean they've left the castle?' I asked.

'No. Vanished!' Mistress Margaret lowered her voice. 'And we all know why.'

'No, we don't.' My head felt like it was stuffed with feathers.

'Because they must be guilty!' she said. 'Who else gains from our good king's death but his sons? Prince Donalbain!'

Yes, I thought. *That* is what I should be thinking. Neither my lady nor Macbeth had anything to gain by the king's death. I could have flown around the castle like the swallows in relief. *Of course* my lady was innocent ...

The grooms must have thought the king's sons would protect them. That was why they hadn't hidden their daggers. But Donalbain and Malcolm had always planned to make the grooms take the blame. They must have drugged the groom's possets ... No, my lady had talked of drugging the grooms last night, *before* the king had been killed.

Perhaps Lord Macbeth had gone to see the king about being made chancellor and had found him dead. The bloody grooms were impossible to wake, and so he'd come back to ask my lady what to do. She would have guessed they must be drugged. But why not wait till morning to seek an audience with the king?

How could the princes have known the grooms wouldn't confess, especially when put to the rack? And it had been Macbeth who'd shut their mouths forever, not the princes. Maybe he'd done it before they could. Or perhaps the grooms had been poisoned and dead already when he struck off their heads.

I looked at the red sauce for the chicken and shuddered.

"'Tis said the princes rode to England,' continued Mistress Margaret eagerly.

'How do you know, if they just vanished?' demanded Mistress Ruth.

'Where else would traitors go?'

Mistress Margaret sat on the cushions again and dipped a piece of bread into the chicken juice. She had not teeth for more. She should have eaten snails, I thought vaguely, like Agnes. And how could she eat at a time like this?

'Good riddance,' said Mistress Ruth. 'Scotland needs no murdering princes.'

Was I mistaken, or did she look relieved too?

I had to stop thinking of 'how' and 'why'. That was the business of lords and ladies, not mine. The important thing was that no matter what I'd heard last night — or had dreamed I'd heard — the princes had proved their guilt. They had killed their father, then left the bloodied daggers on the beds of the drugged grooms. Yes, that worked. Maybe the princes had even asked my lady for a calming posset, then used it on the grooms. And Lord Macbeth had heard a disturbance and come back to ask my lady's advice …

'A foolish plot by foolish boys, sons of a foolish father,' said Mistress Ruth firmly.

She might have been speaking of children in the nursery, yet this was royalty. I glanced at the door, hoping no one had heard.

The poor grooms. Killed not valiantly in battle, but because a beardless lad wanted to be king. A boy who didn't have the courage to stay and bluff his way through all the questions. Had the grooms left wives, or children? I could not truly grieve for Duncan, but for the grooms — servants, just like me — for their wives, like Mam, their children …

Mistress Margaret took a bite of bread and gazed at us, her eyes alight. 'You know what this means, don't you?' she asked softly.

A land left leaderless when the Danes attacked again? I shook my head.

'Why, with the king dead, and the princes guilty of the crime, the Thane of Cawdor must be king.'

Just as I had prophesied. I gaped at her.

Agnes's cottage smelled of peat fire and simmering mutton bones. Warm and comforting, if you ignored the stink of Old Man's Bottom.

'You need some soup,' said Mam, worried.

I shook my head. 'It's not hunger that ails me.'

In truth, I hadn't eaten all day, but from lack of appetite. Nor could I take their food. Not now.

'It's good mutton broth,' said Mam encouragingly.

'Nice and thick, now we finally got oats,' said Agnes.

I had to tell her. Screw my courage to the sticking-place. Where had I heard that?

I heaved my courage up to wherever a sticking-place was. 'Mam, Agnes, I'm sorry. We're leaving tomorrow.'

'We?' asked Mam, while Agnes snapped, 'Where?'

'My lord ... I mean King Macbeth goes to Scone tomorrow to be crowned.'

It sounded strange to put those words together. Stranger still that I had told him up on the heath he'd be king, and now he was. But they had just been words. Stupid words, said by a stupid girl. They had nothing to do with the princes' decision to kill their father.

Mam stared. 'King? Our laird?'

'King!' said Agnes. Her scorn could have melted mutton fat. 'A king's good for two things: getting other people killed or getting killed himself.'

'He rules the country too,' I said.

'He does not! I rules meself. And Rab rules the forge, and old MacWhirtle rules the mill, and Sam Shuteye the sheep on the eastern hill, and Tall Harry those on the west, and —'

'Kings do a different kind of ruling,' I said, before she could name every person in the village. 'My lady must go with him, and her ladies must go with her.'

Mam blinked at me. 'You're going to Scone?' She sounded as desolate as if I'd said I'd be crossing the seas to Ireland.

'To Scone, then Inverness. That's where the king's palace is. I ... I have to go, Mam.'

'No have to about it,' snorted Agnes. 'You come back to the village where you belong.'

'I can't.'

I had sworn myself to my lady's service, and that oath held. Besides, the woman who would be queen had decided I was to be betrothed to Lord Murdoch, though I hadn't told Mam that. Murdoch was sworn to Macbeth. Where he went, so must I.

But did I want to? A sennight past, I'd daydreamed of dancing in a royal castle. Today ... Today I longed for simple things. A cottage. The cat curling around my knees as if she knew there was a cheese in the bag I'd brought.

No, I was a fool. Rags and starvation were simple things. Did I want those too?

And there was another reason I was bound to my lady.

'Agnes, up on the heath,' I began.

'Naught happened,' said Agnes.

'Naught happened,' I agreed. 'But when naught happened, I said Macbeth would be king. And now he is.'

'I told you to keep your head down and do what you were told,' she muttered. 'You know too much now. And that fine lady of yours knows you know it.'

'But you said charms are trickery. Only words.'

I couldn't tell her of the other words I'd heard, or dreamed, during that long night. I must stop thinking about them. The princes had killed the king and laid their daggers by the grooms.

'Charms are words, but I don't know about this "only",' Agnes said. 'I told you, told you over and over. But would you listen? Words have power.'

'And yet they are not magic.'

'No. I warrant it was no magic that stabbed King Duncan, nor spirited off his sons, nor cleaved off the grooms' heads so no one might question them.'

'Macbeth killed the grooms,' I whispered. 'He said he was so horrified at what they'd done, he could not help himself.'

'Come home,' Mam said.

I shook my head.

If the princes were not guilty, then I had caused all this to happen. A foolish girl and foolish words had prompted a man to ... I shut my eyes. I could not even say the words within my head.

Yes, words had power. My words on the heath bound me in guilt to the Macbeths.

Chapter 9

Mam and I talked a while. Words of no matter that mattered more than anything in heart or mind. Memories of Da and things he'd done. The words a mother and daughter say when they know that either might die of spotted fever in a day and the other not be at their bedside. Agnes sat next to the fire, pretending not to listen, checking Paddock for fleas and squishing them between her fingernails.

The shadows grew outside. I must go back to the castle. My lady had given me permission to be away only for the afternoon. But it was as if a thread bound me to Mam, and all I loved. If I went too far away, it might break.

No. I loved my lady too, I told myself. And Lord Murdoch. How could I not love a man so handsome, who treated me like a highborn lady and called my eyes emeralds? And we would be back at Glamis for Christmas. I forced myself to stand up, though I still couldn't let go of Mam's hand.

'My lady has added your name to the list of castle pensioners.' I managed to say. 'A lad will bring you a basket from the castle every Sunday, soups and oats and bannocks.'

'Your ma will get better soup at my hearth, and no stale castle bannocks neither,' grumbled Agnes. 'A decent hunk of venison each week would be more like.'

I finally let go of Mam's hand and turned to her. 'The baskets are for the servants too old to work.'

'Which we are not. Tell them we want a good hunk of venison or a mutton flap, not turnip gruel.'

I shut my eyes for a moment. 'You said I shouldn't draw attention to myself.'

'And dancing off to court with a nearly-queen in a dress so thin it shows your backbone isn't calling attention to yourself? Never mind then. Soup and bannocks it'll have to be.'

'And pies too sometimes. And a goose at Christmas.'

'My word,' said Agnes. 'That *will* make a difference. What mother wouldn't trade her daughter for a few pies and a goose?'

'Agnes, hush,' said Mam. 'I'm glad for Annie. Proud. And you'll be back visiting, won't you now?' She carefully kept the plea from her voice.

'Of course. My lady ... the queen and the king ... will spend Christmas at Glamis if the snow is not too deep to travel, and sometimes we'll be here in the summer when the palace privies have to be cleaned.'

'As long as they don't set you to cleaning privies,' Agnes said.

'Of course not,' said Mam. 'You'll be doing just what you did here, won't you, my lamb? Dressing her ladyship — Her Majesty, I mean — and ... and things like that.'

I had no idea how being a lady-in-waiting to a queen might differ from service to my Lady Macbeth. I wasn't even sure what a queen actually did. But I nodded.

'Yes, things like that. I ... I'm to be carried in a curtained litter to Scone too, with my lady ... Her Majesty —'

'On one of them bed things?' Agnes said scornfully. 'Your legs will drop off, girl, if you don't use them.'

No chance of that with all the stairs in castles. I wondered if Agnes had ever climbed a staircase. And what would she say if I told her that from today Annie Grasseyes was Lady Anne?

I stood. Paddock jumped off Agnes's lap and twisted around my ankles. 'I must get back to the castle and see that her ladyship's — I mean Her Majesty's — dresses are packed properly.'

'So young to be a queen,' said Mam wonderingly.

Agnes gazed at the fire. 'The young queens are the worst.'

'You've never known a young queen,' I said wearily. 'You haven't even met a queen.'

'Nor do I want to. But I know young girls. Girls like you spouting words about kings when you weren't supposed to. I saw what happened when old Graeme the shepherd took a young wife. "I must have a lambskin cloak," she whimpered. "I must have cobbler's shoes." Afore the end of the season he'd sold near half his flock. And when Jan the miller wed that girl young as his oldest granddaughter, she told him, "Put the lower field into rye," and then it got the rust and poisoned every bag ground at the mill and the whole village went barking mad all autumn.'

'I never heard that,' said Mam.

'A long time ago. And them as could talk about it all died because of it.'

Then how do you know about it? I thought.

'Young girls want to change the world. And if they're pretty enough and wilful enough, sometimes they can.'

'What's wrong with that?' I challenged her. 'The world needs changing. Duncan was a terrible king with all his wars, demanding so much of the harvest every year to feed his army and build his ships.'

'That's true,' said Mam.

Agnes raised a shaggy eyebrow. 'So King Duncan deserved to be murdered?'

'Of course not.'

She stared at me. 'Why not? What's the death of one king and a pair of grooms compared to thousands in his armies?'

'I ... I don't know.'

My heart still bled at the thought of the poor grooms, sacrificed for ambition, their families not just grieving but having to bear the whispers of those who wondered if the grooms had been guilty.

'I'll tell you then.' Of course she would. 'The land has to have rules. And one of them is you don't chop off a guest's head. No one could travel safe if people went around chopping off their guests' heads. And you don't break promises neither.'

Sometimes she made sense. I'd been tossing this over in my mind and here was Agnes, a crone from the village, handing the answer to me on a platter. Everyone at the castle that night had sworn loyalty to the king. They had broken their oath like a plate smashed on the hearth.

I met her gaze. 'So if ... if you were going to kill someone, you'd challenge them openly?'

'Annie!' said Mam. 'What a thing to ask.'

Agnes laughed. 'Course not. I'd smile and smile then poison their pottage the next morning. And no one would ever know they'd been poisoned neither.'

'But you said —'

'You said *if*. If I *had* to kill. And I don't, and never have, so don't you go looking at me like that. *If* I did, it'd be because some scunner was trying to kill me or one I loves, and that was the only way to keep them safe. I don't hold with killing the way some folks do. Them as creeps around my cottage door at night whispering, "Oh, my poor father-in-law, in so much pain. Death would be a kindness really." If a man's screaming in pain, I'll give him something to take the pain away, to make him sleep. But only sleep.' She gazed at me steadily. 'There's some as may question that. But there's one thing everyone in this village will agree with. You don't kill someone just because you want to take their place.'

'I … I told Macbeth he would be king,' I whispered.

Agnes peered at me for so long that I bent to pat Paddock just to escape her gaze.

'If he believed you,' she said eventually, 'he could have waited till he was. But you said the princes killed the king. That's what the whole village is saying.'

'Surely you don't think …' began Mam. She shook her head. 'Lord Macbeth has been a good thane to this village. And his lady has been gracious to us. Taking you in up at the castle, and providing baskets for the poor.'

'If he hadn't led the men to war, there'd be no poor,' said Agnes.

'Those were King Duncan's wars,' I said.

'What really matters,' said Mam quietly, 'is that the new king is kind. Lord Macbeth is a kind man, isn't he? And her ladyship?'

Was Macbeth kind? He wasn't *un*kind. And Murdoch had sworn loyalty to him. Surely Murdoch wouldn't have given his oath if Macbeth hadn't deserved it? And her ladyship had been good to me. But kind?

'Truly, I must go now.'

I wouldn't cry. Crying would make Mam think I wasn't happy and she'd worry. Or worry more than usual. And I was happy. A place at court, and Murdoch would be made an earl; and I was going to ride in a litter like … like a countess.

Agnes sighed. 'Well, if you must go.' She fumbled in a tall basket woven from marsh grass, then handed me a grubby flask. 'Goose fat and buttonwort. I hear Inverness is a terror of a place for congestion of the lungs. Rub this on your chest every morning and it'll keep you safe.'

Safe from anyone coming closer than half a league more like. But I nodded and placed the flask in the bag at my waist. I hugged her awkwardly. I'd never hugged her before. After a moment she hugged me back. She smelled of sour peat and bitter herbs and something else that was hers entirely.

I hugged Mam then, and the hug went on and on, our tears mingling despite my fine intentions.

She broke away before I did. 'You'd better go. You don't want to be late for a nearly-queen.'

I stumbled out, my tears a veil I could barely see through.

I'd gone a dozen paces when someone called, 'Annie!' Rab. He must have been waiting for me.

I nodded politely and kept walking. I didn't want him to see my tears.

Suddenly he was beside me. 'You need a handkerchief.' Then, 'What's that stench?'

I fumbled in my bag and pulled out the flask. It had leaked.

'Agnes's goose-fat salve.'

He grinned. 'There are brave men in this village, but none brave enough to contract congestion of the lungs and face Agnes's goose-fat salve. Here, wipe your eyes on my kilt.' He held it up. 'And blow your nose too.'

'Not on your kilt!'

'Why not?' he replied mildly. 'There's nothing in your nose that's worse than what comes off a horse's hoof or from its backside.'

'Thank you,' I said. 'I don't want to blow my nose in horse droppings.'

He laughed. 'Here, the bit within the fold is clean enough. Blow.'

I did. And felt better.

'Now, what's the trouble?' he asked as we began to walk again.

'No trouble.' I hesitated. The whole of Scotland would know it soon. 'We leave tomorrow for Scone for Lord Macbeth to be crowned king. Me too.'

'I see,' he said slowly.

'Lord Macbeth will be a good king,' I said. 'He's a warrior, strong where Duncan was weak. And he's seen what battle brings. He won't attack England each summer, like a child trying to take more than his fair share of bannock.'

Rab gave me a sharp glance. 'You've learned much up at the castle.'

We walked a while in silence. I wondered what he did see. He was no fool, Big Rab McPherson.

'Do you want to go?' he asked at last.

'Of course! To see the palace, and Inverness, and visitors from foreign lands.'

I was trying to convince myself, not him. He knew it.

'How long are you bound to her ladyship?' he asked quietly.

'I … I don't know. It's not like an apprenticeship with a contract that you sign.'

I'd always thought I'd leave service when I married. But queens had married ladies to attend them, those whose husbands attended the king. *Would* she let me leave if I asked her to release me? She liked me. She trusted me. Had trusted me beyond anyone in the kingdom. That alone might make her hold me close. Only I knew that she'd asked for a charm to make her husband Thane of Cawdor. She and I seemed bound by the same fate now, one maybe of my making …

'You're troubled,' said Rab.

I nodded. That seemed to sum it up.

'Then stay.'

'I can't.'

I thought he'd argue. But he nodded. 'Each of us must do our duty.'

'And yet you didn't go to battle for Glamis.'

'It's not to Glamis that I owe my duty. Don't worry, Annie, I'll keep my eye on your mam. I've got enough peat dried for her and Agnes for this winter, and my apprentices will repair their thatch as soon as the harvest is in. I'll write to you each week.'

The minister at the kirk taught boys to read for a penny each on Sunday afternoons and I knew Rab had learned. But paper to write on once a week was a terrible extravagance.

'You're a good friend, Rab. I'd value a letter.'

I'd need to ask Mistress — no, *Lady* Ruth — for more lessons so I could read them.

'Then it's done.' He smiled at me. 'And here's your castle. I'd better be getting back to the forge afore the apprentices try to shoe the hens. One tried to shoe a sheep last week.'

'Did he manage it?'

'It bit him. He's been hiding the wound ever since.'

'No wonder. Bitten by a sheep!'

I was almost at the drawbridge before I realised Rab

McPherson had left me smiling on a day when I thought I'd never smile again.

We left the next morning as dawn was cracking yellow like an egg. I wasn't sure how you got into a litter. I watched how her ladyship did it, sitting on it like it was a bed then lifting up her legs, and did the same. The curtains dropped. Suddenly we were in a world of two. The litter began to move, rolling back and forth as if the men weren't quite in step.

'What are you thinking?' asked my lady.

No, the queen. Agnes was right. It felt odd to have a girl almost my own age as queen. But this girl had been married three years, had borne a son and lost him, had watched her husband go to battle and urged him to …

'I was wondering if a ship feels like this, rolling back and forth,' I said instead.

'Much rougher. And much less safe.'

I had forgotten that her father's estate bordered the sea, and her mother had gone a-Viking too. She must have been in boats a hundred times.

'What is the sea like?'

'Big. You'll see it for yourself soon. What is the gossip at the castle?' she added abruptly.

I didn't pretend not to know what she meant. 'That Prince Donalbain and Prince Malcolm ordered the grooms to kill the king; or killed the king themselves and made it look as if the grooms had done it. They poisoned the grooms after the deed was done, which was why they lay drugged when my lord ... I mean King Macbeth ... found them. Others say ...' I hesitated.

'Well?'

'That witches enchanted the grooms so they could not move once they had done the deed.'

'Witches for good then, not evil,' she said calmly. 'Making sure those responsible for such a vile deed were punished.'

'Yes, ma'am,' I said. Mistress ... Lady Margaret had said that was what we must call the queen now.

She lay back on the cushions. 'It is time Scotland had a queen.'

I nodded. Duncan's wife had died at Malcolm's birth.

'What do queens do, ma'am?'

I thought of Agnes saying young girls thought they could change the world.

'Scotland hasn't had one in my time or yours,' she said slowly. 'But I have read of queens who led armies while their husbands were away crusading in the Holy Land or fighting elsewhere.'

Her voice had none of the eagerness of a few days ago — had it been so recently? — when she had raged that she wished to be part of the battle too.

'Do you want to command an army, ma'am?'

'No,' she said quietly. 'Not now.'

'What else do queens do?'

'Much the same as the lady of the castle, I expect. Make sure important visitors are made happy. See to the comfort of their husbands and their people. Weave the threads of politics into a fine tapestry, give counsel to the king. I think, perhaps, a queen may find much more to do if she has a mind for it. But we shall see.'

I remembered Mam's words. 'And be kind to her subjects, ma'am?'

She laughed, the tension in her body relaxing. 'I do not think the most courteous courtier would call me kind. But I will be a good queen. I will swear to that.'

I could hear the truth in her words. Part of me that had been poised like a frightened hare, ready to run, relaxed.

'And there will be a grand coronation to come, ma'am,' I said, trying to keep her mood bright.

Suddenly her laughter was gone. 'Yes. The coronation. It will be grand enough. The problem is, who will come to it?'

'I don't understand, my lady ... ma'am.'

'Macbeth was cousin to King Duncan, and Cawdor is the biggest estate in Scotland. But there will be some who think that Donalbain should be king now that his father is dead.'

'Even though he ... he killed his father? And is fled to England?'

'A prince is a prince as long as he lives.' She made an obvious attempt to change the subject. 'We must be passing the village now. Shall we have the curtains open so you may say farewell to what was once your life?'

'Thank you, ma'am.'

I pulled the curtains back and there they were, just down the hill. Mam and Agnes, standing ankle-deep in drifting fog, Rab next to them.

I waved.

Mam waved back. So did Rab, then put his arm around Mam as her body shook with sobs. Agnes didn't wave. But her glare softened into something that might, in someone else, have meant she was trying not to show her tears.

Then we were past.

'A fine young man,' said the queen. 'Is he your brother?'

'No. But he cares for my mother as if he were.'

The men tramped down the hill, taking the litter with them. I craned to keep looking, but the fog swirled thicker.

And Mam and Agnes and Rab were gone.

Chapter 10

Lord Macbeth was crowned king on Caislean Credi at Scone, sitting on the Stone of Destiny.

It rained.

It had rained since the afternoon we set out from Glamis. Grey rain, soft rain, that crept stealthily into every crevice so you didn't know how much had fallen till each small drop combined. The men trudged through mud as wet as themselves, and damp seeped through the leather curtains of our litter. Burns grew to streams, streams to rivers, rivers to flood.

Perhaps the autumn floods were why so few thanes arrived to witness the archbishop anointing the new king. I hoped that was the reason. My lady said nothing, but I could see her counting who was here, and who was not.

The servants had to change my sodden dress before the coronation feast. I had servants to pin me too now, into a yellow silk dress, and golden sleeves and a bodice so tight

I could hardly breathe — though we three still dressed the queen. She wore gold brocade, with scarlet trim, and scarlet sleeves and petticoat. She looked a true queen, and she proceeded with the king into the banqueting hall, with the chief lords and ladies of the court behind them. I walked arm in arm with Lord Murdoch, Lady Ruth and Lady Margaret cooing at the sight of us as they walked on the arms of lesser knights.

The banquet was a fine one. Course after course, so many I could not count them, as well as a brace of cleverly contrived cockatrices so grand that everyone exclaimed over them, a pig's head sewn onto a capon with a sheep's tail sewn onto that, and jellies and compotes and marzipan fancies. I stopped eating after the third course, and played with plover pastry on my plate. Lady Ruth ate every course and had a stomach-ache for two days afterwards.

The queen sat, straight and gracious, smiling, offering the choice meats to her husband. He smiled too, but it seemed painted on his face. His eyes shifted uneasily about the hall, as if he expected the princes to jump out from behind the tapestries and demand the crown. But it was his now. Definite word had come from England that they were headed to the English court.

After the fruits and nuts and fancies were served, the king formally touched Murdoch and Macbeth's other men on each shoulder with his sword, naming each of them earls — the first that Scotland had ever had — giving them precedence over every thane in all the land.

Murdoch strode to me afterwards, to where I sat above the salt now, as one of the queen's ladies. 'Will you dance with me, kind lady?' he asked, bowing, his eyes already dancing.

'I will only dance with an earl today,' I said demurely. 'Can you find me one?'

He looked around, then down at himself. 'Why, perchance, there is one here. Will you take my hand, my lady?'

I smiled, stood and curtseyed. 'Most willingly, my lord.'

'And may I keep that hand, to have and to hold?'

'Yes, my lord,' I said. I didn't know if this was a proposal, not when our marriage had been arranged for us. But the women on either side smiled and laughed, and the men held up their tankards in a cheer.

My heart beat as loudly as the drums as he held my hand lightly to the dance floor. We moved into the set with the other dancers. Mistress — *Lady* Margaret had taught me many dances, but this was the first time I had danced with a man as my partner, and with the whole court looking on.

We formed a line. Suddenly I realised Murdoch and I were at the head of it. He was an earl and I was a queen's lady now, the most important dancers on the floor. And

I *was* in a golden dress, or nearly. He smiled at me. 'It seems we are to lead, my lady.' He took my hands.

It was a simple dance, thank goodness, designed to be a courtly display for royalty to watch rather than a way to pass a long winter night. He and I skipped down the line, one of my hands taking the hand of every man in turn, while he took the hand of every woman, while my other kept hold of his.

At the end of the line he kissed my hand. 'You dance most beautifully, my lady.'

His lips were warm. I flushed, unsure what to say. He laughed as the next couple skipped towards us. 'As your hand is mine, I may kiss it whenever I like.'

'Of course, my lord,' I said, blushing.

'Perhaps we should rename Greymouth. For how can it be Greymouth when my lady's lips are rose?'

I tried to think of a witty answer, but luckily we were swirled into the dance once more.

He kissed my hand again as he handed me back to my seat.

'*My lady's hand is almond white*
Her lips are like a rose,
Soon I the luckiest of knights
When my knight her nights knows,' he recited.

More cooing and applause at his cleverness. He smiled modestly. 'Until tomorrow, my lady,' he promised. I watched him stride back to the top of the table to talk with the king. He always said 'my lady', I realised, had never once used my name.

'My name is Annie,' I said softly. But even those on either side were applauding the music, and no one heard.

Autumn sent the trees shaggy with gold and red, like banners proclaiming the new king. The rains cleared enough to bring in a harvest, but the rivers still ran high. No other thanes arrived to kneel to King Macbeth in fealty. That must wait till spring.

The days limped past at the palace. My time changed little. There were more stairs to climb in Inverness's Cawdor Castle than Glamis; a stronger stench from the town chamber pots, mixed with the salt of the sea. I would have liked to climb along the coast and see the endless blue reach to the horizon, or explore a proper town and take a basket to the markets, but of course each day I must attend the queen. I still helped dress her in the morning, and again at dinner time and evening, grander cloth and jewels every day, but still much the same to pin. We brushed her hair and sewed at tapestries, sitting quietly on our cushions below the throne, as colourful in our silks as tapestries ourselves, when she was holding an audience with petitioners or the king.

I had thought Macbeth would be triumphant, striding the corridors of the palace. But affairs of state weighed heavier than any battle. His eyes looked smudged with coal; his cheeks sank like a village crone's in a hard winter. It seemed that winter sprinkled his hair with grey snow too. There was no time for hunting or tournaments this season. Macbeth had harvested a kingdom, and now must tend it, sending messengers and gifts to woo the families who had not attended the coronation. Murdoch was his chief messenger. I hardly saw Murdoch after the coronation feast where he had claimed my hand. King Macbeth sent ambassadors to England too, to demand the princes be returned and tried for their crime; to Paris and Rome, making or sealing allegiances I tried to understand.

My lady ... Her Majesty stayed at her husband's side even during audiences, offering him soft counsel for the petitioners that came to him to decide between two claimants for an estate, or who should have the grazing rights to a field or half a mountain. Even when the king met with the chancellor she was there, gracious, charming, keeping the threads of Scotland in her hands as easily as she'd sewn her tapestry.

The king needed her there, though none dared say it aloud. Time and time again he hesitated, or did not seem to remember what a petitioner had said a short time before. It was as if part of him were elsewhere, at Glamis, perhaps, or reliving the tragedies that had led him to his throne. Perhaps, indeed, he was made to lead troops, and not to govern a kingdom.

But not the queen. She seemed to have been made for a high estate, wise in judgement, seeming tireless as she judged the owner of the piglets that one man's sow had born, but another's boar had sired. She was not ambitious for her husband now, but for the whole of Scotland, to be a land of plenty and of peace — and no rebellion should mar the rule of King Macbeth.

At night, she had bad dreams.

I slept in the truckle bed next to her every night now. The first night she had woken, screaming, Lady Margaret had been with her, and made such a fuss calling for a posset and lavender oil to calm her that half the castle waked, and wondered at the noise. The next night, Her Majesty asked for me.

I had slept next to Mam, on the bracken bed at Agnes's, when she woke, sobbing from her dreams where Da strode in, smiling and alive. I knew warm arms and a soothing voice would frighten nightmares, because Mam soothed me too, when memories of that winter when our only food for three days was a frozen turnip flooded back to me in dreams.

I did not dream of frozen turnips now. There would be no starvation for Lady Anne, attendant to the queen, nor the Countess of Greymouth when the queen decided Lord Murdoch and I should wed. Daggers decorated my dreams instead, oozing blood; the headless grooms walking the ramparts of Glamis

Castle; Duncan roaming the halls, gore dripping from his wounds.

Often when the queen woke it was a relief for me to wake too. I kneeled on the floor, holding her hand, making myself smell the sweet apple wood of the castle fires instead of smouldering peat; listen to the bells toll the hour and the watchman cry 'all's well'.

And all *was* well, I told myself. Macbeth was king. The story was complete, or would be when I was wed, the birth of my children and grandchildren the only adventures still to come. All the horrors had been back at Glamis ...

It almost made me wish that we weren't going back there for Christmas. But, as I shared the queen's litter again, every step the bearers took seemed to make me more myself again, as if a shadow inhabited my skin at Inverness, a stranger called Lady Anne.

It felt so deeply right to be back in the village again, to feel Mam's arms around me, to have Paddock purring on my knee and expecting to have her ears stroked. Even Agnes's glares seemed comfortable. Somehow the village was still the centre of the world for me, far more than the palace of all Scotland in Inverness. It was as if my life was a tapestry that had hung hooked on the wall all my time away.

Rab had cared for Mam and Agnes just as he'd promised. The thatch was newly mended, the peat dried and stacked under the eaves. The baskets they received from the castle had been more lavish than the other pensioners got too, with meat every week and cheese as well as butter. Mam looked almost plump, and even Agnes looked less like a black-clad broom. The queen repaid loyalty.

She even gave me permission to spend the entire feast day at the cottage. I brought Mam a bolt of red flannel from Inverness to make petticoats. Agnes scoffed at the colour, but later during our visit I saw a flash of red under her dress. She stewed the goose from the castle with herbs that tasted far better than Old Man's Bottom, and I brought butter cake, which needed the castle's oven to bake, and marzipan fruits.

I laughed as Mam wondered at the tiny apples, plums and quinces. I sat there on the bracken-stuffed wool cushion, happier than I'd been for half a year, even though I dressed in velvet now, and had a fox fur cloak to shield me from the cold with a silver brooch to clasp it, a gift from my Lord Murdoch.

He wasn't with us this Christmas, but on an embassy to France. I wished him safe on the winter seas and counted the days till his return. No date had been set for our wedding, nor had the banns been read. 'I do not want to lose you so soon,' the queen had told me frankly. 'And I would, as soon as you were breeding.'

Murdoch had kissed me when we said farewell — my first kiss, and I'd liked it. There were no scenes of passionate adoration between us, like in the stories Lady Margaret read to us as we stitched. Lord Murdoch paid me compliments, and kissed my hand, and taught me new dances most kindly, not laughing when I lost my place. This, it seemed, was what the highborn expected of a marriage. My lady hadn't even met Macbeth when they were first betrothed.

'More goose?' offered Agnes, piling it into my bowl. 'You're a wisp of a cloud still. And your head still in the clouds too. You need some fat upon your bones.'

'My bones do well enough,' I said. 'Oh, Mam, I wish you had seen the roast ox at the banquet for the French ambassador. It took ten men to carry it in, and its hide was polished and its horns gilded. The king cleft it with his sword and out fell sausages!'

'Never say you've met a Frenchman!' said Mam.

'Lots of them. They talk strangely, but they are most polite. The queen has a French cook now to make her sauces.'

'What's a sauce?' asked Agnes.

'A covering for plain meat, like gravy in a stew but made separate.'

'The best of meat is in the bones. Why would someone want the gravy made separate? Foreigners have funny ways.'

'I've seen a monkey too,' I said.

'What's that?' asked Mam eagerly.

'A small animal, much like a man but covered in fur, and it capers on the ground.'

Mam looked dubious. 'Sounds heathen. Does a monkey go to kirk and say the prayers?'

'Well, no.'

'Then it's heathen,' said Mam firmly, not looking at Agnes, who went to kirk but twice a year and that just to stop the whispers getting too loud.

The door darkened with Rab's bulk.

'Come in!' cried Mam. 'There's a good goose stew in the pot, and bannocks hot on the hearth.'

'Your bannocks or your Annie's?' asked Rab. He sat on the cushion beside me, the flames dancing on his face. 'It's good to see you, Annie.'

'And good to see you,' I said.

He'd written every week, as he'd said he would, but not the kind of letter I'd expected, as long as Murdoch's poems. Rab's were just three words, *All is well*, scratched on scraps of paper with old accounts on the other side. But it had comforted me to get them, to know that, indeed, all was well.

'I made you all gifts,' he said, and produced them from his kirtle: three finely wrought iron cloak pins. Mine was a five-petalled rose; Mam's a deer; and Agnes's a thistle, not the flower, but a thorny leaf.

Agnes laughed. 'You've got me right, lad!' She fastened it to her dress. 'The hag of thistles. That's me.'

I'd taken my cloak off, thanks to the warmth of the good peat fire, and was glad Murdoch's silver pin was hidden in the folds. 'It's lovely, Rab.' And strange to think his big hands could do such fine work.

'A change from swords and ploughs and horseshoes.' He took the bowl of stew from Mam. 'Smells good.'

'Better than your Maggie Two-Teeth could make,' said Agnes. 'The secret's in the herbs.'

'Not such a secret,' said Mam, 'for I know it now, and so does Annie.'

'A secret between three is still a secret,' Agnes said, giving first Mam and then me a sharp eye. 'Eat up, lad. There's butter cake as well, and if we don't eat it the cat will get at it, and he's fat enough already.'

Mam laughed. And I sat next to her, and to Rab, warm by the fire, as Mam showed him the marvel of marzipan fruits, and I knew this was a jewel of a day that would glow bright for my whole life, brighter than any ruby in Macbeth's crown.

Chapter 11

We laboured through snowdrifts back to Inverness. The day was fine when we set out, but the grey clouds grew heavier and, finally, the snow fell. I felt guilty to be warm inside the curtained litter with the queen while the men who carried us stumbled through the drifts. The queen spoke little, though she had been gay all through the Christmas revels. I listened to the men's leather-clad feet tramp and slip, all other sounds lost in the snow, and tried not to think of all the bloody deeds crammed into the past year. Instead I contemplated the year to come.

I had hoped that the king would recover his spirits at Glamis, where he had been boy, man and thane. But he started at every shadow as the torches flickered in the corridors, and shuddered each time winter's wind moaned and rubbed against the castle, as if it were a dragon ghost sent to snare us.

But he would be better when summer came, I told myself. Many felt dark-spirited in the short dim days of winter. When summer spread its gold across the land, our king would smile once more too. Good harvests and, God willing, no raiders from the north.

'A good snow means a good harvest,' said the queen.

I stared at her. Had she heard my thoughts? But what else would a queen be thinking of at the beginning of a year?

'And with my husband king, no raiders will attack our land,' she added. 'The Norsemen will be afraid to face a warrior king.'

'Scotland is lucky to have such a one,' I said.

'And hopefully this year all will acknowledge it.'

It was hard to read her expression in the dim light.

'Don't worry, ma'am. Surely the thanes will come to swear allegiance when the passes are clear once more,' I said.

She smiled at that. 'No one except you and the chancellor presumes to give advice to a queen.'

I flushed. I'd spent too much time with Agnes.

The queen laughed. 'No, I like it. Words can be angels to a listener's ear. You are discreet enough to talk when only I can hear.'

And the men carrying the litter, I thought. But that was gentlefolk: they never saw the man who carried the water, or the foot soldier who was one-armed because of battle.

'You miss Lord Murdoch?' she asked.

'Yes, Your Majesty.' I might not love him as Mam and Da had loved each other, but he brightened the long days. 'But I am grateful for the honour of the king sending him as ambassador to France.'

'Let us pray that he succeeds.'

'He didn't tell me why he went, ma'am.'

Her mouth quirked, amused. 'I am glad to hear it. His mission is for the ears of the French king alone, not a big-eyed chit who prompts her queen for answers.'

'I'm sorry, ma'am.'

She laughed. 'You don't look it. Of course you're curious.' She paused, then added, almost to herself, 'And I do trust you. Murdoch was sent for this: to give assurances to the French king that the old alliance stands firm. Scotland will not attack the lands of France, nor France look covetously on ours.'

'The French king will agree to this, ma'am?'

'Of course. He gains nothing by denying it. But Murdoch had another quest: to ask the French to aid us should attack come from England. In turn, we will offer our assistance when they next fight the English.'

'Do the French fight the English often, ma'am?'

Another laugh. 'As regularly as we sing matins.'

'Then the French king must agree.'

'It is not so simple. France's power is great, ours small. It is said their army is so vast it reaches to the horizon, a city full of knights on horseback, a forest of spears behind. Their help to us would be an elephant striding down the hills; ours but a bee that buzzes near its foot.'

I tried to imagine an army as big as that. I'd seen Macbeth's army march away, so many men it took half the morning to watch them pass. And I knew the king's army held a score of legions just as large, if all the lords answered the call to bring their men and swords.

Suddenly I grasped the import of her earlier words. 'England, ma'am? Do you think they will attack us?'

'Duncan's son, Malcolm, is at the English court,' she said flatly. I noticed she did not call him prince.

'And Donalbain too?'

'It seems Donalbain had an accident on the road. A dangerous country, England.'

'You think Malcolm is asking the English king for an army to attack us?'

'I am quite sure of it. But if France announces that it will fight for Scotland, the English will be deaf to Malcolm's pleas.'

'If he deserved the throne, he should have stayed and claimed it,' I said.

She nodded. 'His flight proclaimed his guilt. Malcolm must have scarce blood enough in all his sickly veins to give a sheet a stain. If I were him, I would have galloped to each thane, convinced them of my innocence and gathered in the harvest of their men. Instead he fled, a puppy battered by a broom.'

I remembered the strong-eyed young man watching Macbeth on the morning of his father's death. He did not seem a coward. 'And if the French refuse to help us, ma'am? Could we defeat the English?'

I thought of all the battles King Duncan had lost. But he had been the invader then, his army tired and hungry by the time it reached the English forces. This time it would be their army that must march for weeks or months to meet ours.

'We will win, with my husband at the army's head — if he stays bold and resolute, and if all the thanes are loyal.'

I hesitated. 'Are they loyal, ma'am?'

She gave me a glance as sharp as Agnes's. 'Aye, there's the rub. What reels will our great thanes dance to when they hear the pipes of war?'

She gazed at the swinging curtains of the litter as if she could see all of Scotland beyond their dampness.

'Surely the thanes would not fight for Malcolm,' I said. 'Not for a man who killed his father.'

'No. But they may not fight for us either.' She met my eyes. 'It is so easy to say, oh, the river flooded, we could not cross; or, the fog descended and we could not see and so we missed the battle. But if my husband stands firm, then the thanes will stand with him.'

And if he does not? I thought.

The curtains parted. I saw snow, and a man's face pinched and blue. 'The abbey is just up yonder hill, Your Majesty.'

The stones that seemed to weight her fell away. She smiled at him, a gracious queen. 'I'll warrant you are gladder still than I. Thank you for this safe passage, and thank your men from me.'

'I will, Your Majesty.' The curtain dropped.

The queen turned to me. 'It is time to wear a public face. Come, tend to my hair.'

'French flowers for a Scottish rose!'

I looked up from the tapestry. 'Lord Murdoch! I did not know you had returned.'

Two months had passed. The briars still hadn't bloomed upon the hills of Inverness, nor the well-bred roses in the castle gardens. Lady Ruth, Lady Margaret and I had begun a grand tapestry for the queen's chamber, the most exciting thing to happen in the long dark days, for few ventured on the winter seas to Inverness, or across the snowy roads and ice-cracked streams. Today Lady Ruth checked the castle linen, while Lady Margaret inspected the hams and cheese, to make sure they were well stored. One day I'd need to spend my time doing the same, at Greymouth, but today I was glad to leave the tasks to them.

I rose from my cushion — it had taken me many lessons to learn how to stand up elegantly while trussed in the close-fitting bodice demanded at court — and curtseyed perfectly as he bowed low.

He laughed. 'One winter rose all alone in the solar? And I the luckiest gardener to pluck it.'

'Her Majesty has just left to attend the king. She bade me stay here till she returned.' I had wondered why she didn't want an attendant.

His face clouded. 'I know. I have just had speech with Their Majesties.'

'Your ... mission ... did not go well?' I asked tentatively.

He raised an eyebrow. It was a different shape from when he'd left. He must have plucked it, after the fashion of the French court. 'You know of my mission, my lady?'

I flushed. 'Her Majesty did me the honour ...'

'I am glad you have her trust. Man and wife should have no secrets between them. That cushion looks most comfortable,' he hinted.

'Sir, will you sit?'

It still seemed odd to be giving an earl permission to sit. I caught his scent — of spices and some unfamiliar flower. I was glad he wanted to talk to me. I wanted to be the kind of wife who shared a man's thoughts, not just his bed and care of his estates.

'The mission was ... indifferent won,' he said. 'The Heart of France received me most kindly, and made diverse offers of brotherhood and friendship to our king. Yet they were but feathers in the air, not an arrow to our needs.'

Or in commoner's words: the French king had smiled and been polite, but hadn't committed his army to help us if England attacked.

'But shall we talk of happier matters?' He smiled at me. 'Here are your flowers.'

Suddenly there was something in his hand: a necklace of brilliant stones, the centrepiece a bloom of red and gold. I almost gaped at it. Were those rubies, and for me?

'I ... I do not have words to thank my lord ...'

'What better thanks than for my lady to be so glad that she is speechless?' The smile came back to his face. 'Her Majesty vows you are not usually so short of speech.'

I flushed again. 'I ... I talk too much.'

'How so, when your words trill like the lark yet have the wisdom of a chancellor? The winters at Greymouth are long and dark, as its name,' he added. 'A cheering tongue will be most welcome.'

I wondered if he knew when we would be married, or if he too waited for the queen to announce it. Would it be overly bold to ask?

He took my hand and kissed it. His lips were warm and the pleasant spice scent became stronger, though probably not strong enough to ward off a congestion of the lungs. I almost grinned. Agnes's salve lay up in my room, wrapped ten times to hide the smell. I couldn't bear to throw it out.

'How goes the king?' asked Murdoch, too casually.

'Most king-like,' I answered carefully.

'He seemed ... weary when he gave me audience.'

Murdoch wasn't the only one to have noticed the shadows under Macbeth's eyes. Our king's shoulders were broad, but were they strong enough to bear the weight of all Scotland?

'I asked if, now the winter snows are vanishing from the Highlands, he planned to ride to the thanes who have not yet pledged to him,' said Murdoch quietly. He met my eyes. 'Her Majesty said yes at the same time that His Majesty shrugged and said he did not know.'

What should I answer? I couldn't tell him that Her Majesty muttered in her sleep, or screamed with nightmares, and did not sleep at all sometimes until night's candles guttered in their holders.

To my relief Murdoch smiled again. 'Will my lady wear my gift this afternoon at the banquet?'

'With joy in my heart, my lord, both at the gift and that the giver be back and far from hungry waves.' I let my grin show. 'And far from French roses who might try to catch him with their thorns.'

He laughed. 'No thorn caught me in fair France, not when the fairest flower of all waited for me in Scotland.' He raised my hand to his lips and kissed it. 'Till the banquet.'

After he had gone, I looked at the necklace in my lap, suddenly realising that it wasn't just a gift to me, but also to the betrothed of the Earl of Greymouth. Would Murdoch expect our daughter to wear it too, or our daughter-in-law to come? Lady Margaret would know.

The Great Hall was decorated as carefully as we of the court were dressed. The tapestries were still those of Duncan's time, but the great Macbeth banner with two swords crossed above two hands joined hung above the high table, with smaller painted banners about the walls. Fires tended day and night made the hall warm enough for ladies to leave their cloaks, showing bare arms and low necklines that would have had Agnes muttering about hussies, if she had seen us.

A hundred wax candles glowed in the holders above us, and in the sconces around the walls, almost as bright as summer's light. Jewels glinted at wrists and necks, my necklace among them. Silks brushed satin, lace and French brocade. I wore a rich fabric of rose and gold that Murdoch had brought back. It had taken six maids and Lady Margaret's supervision to have the dress ready for tonight.

My heavy brocade skirts swished against the flagstones as we swept in behind the king and queen. I wished that Mam could see us.

The queen was dressed in her favourite scarlet, with rose-red sleeves and paler underskirts. I had scarcely seen her in another colour since ... since the night I tried to forget, back in Glamis. She'd even had us dye her nightshifts red.

The first course sat already upon the table. I sighed, knowing it had probably sat there since early morn. The roasted lambs, so elegantly arranged on beds of greens with a meringue of wool, would be cold and greasy, the soup tepid. The salmon jelly, which sat nearest the fireplace, was beginning to ooze juice. Highborn folk might have all the meat and ale they wished for, and fancies such as peacocks' tongues and lemon possets, but they rarely enjoyed the luxury all cottagers knew — food fresh and hot from its cooking.

We stood next to the table, waiting for His Majesty to bid us sit and eat. But he just stood there, lost in thought.

The queen placed her hand upon his shoulder. 'My royal lord ...'

'What?' He seemed to notice her, and us, still standing and waiting for him.

The queen smiled, trying to put him, and us, at ease. 'You do not give the cheer. The sauce to meat is ceremony; meeting were bare without it.'

Macbeth managed a smile for his wife. 'Sweet remembrancer!'

His eyes looked as though they were smudged with soot. He seemed thinner than last summer, though in a padded doublet it was hard to tell. I wondered how fierce the threat from England was, and glanced about the hall, counting the thanes who supped with us. Four strangers and their men, which meant, I hoped, four more who'd come to swear allegiance to their new king.

The king turned to the court. 'Now, good digestion wait on appetite, and health on both!'

'May it please Your Highness to sit?' asked Lord Lennox, bowing him to his seat.

We all sat, then realised that the king still stood. This was awkward. Some men made to rise; others waved their hands at them to sit again. The court couldn't jump up and down at table like a salmon in a brook. Besides, he'd formally made us welcome.

Macbeth surveyed the hall. 'Were the graced person of our Banquo present, our pleasure would be roofed,' he said slowly.

I glanced around. Lord Banquo wasn't in his accustomed seat. My stomach growled. I'd eaten nothing since the sun rose. I wished the king would sit down and take a mouthful so we could begin to eat. But he stood chatting to Lord Lennox and the Earl of Ross.

I caught Murdoch's eye and touched the necklace at my throat. He discreetly touched his fingers to his lips and blew the kiss to me.

Suddenly the hall was silent. Even the rustle of silk on silk ceased. I looked back at the high table and saw the king staring at his own vacant seat.

'The table's full,' he muttered, glaring at Lord Lennox.

Lennox looked puzzled. 'Here is a place reserved, sir.'

'Where?' Macbeth demanded.

'Here, my good lord.' Lennox hesitated as the king still failed to sit down.

Macbeth's eyes widened. He lurched back with a cry as if he'd seen a hound from hell.

'What is it that moves Your Highness?' Lennox cried.

Macbeth gazed around at us. 'Which of you has done this?' he screamed. The sound echoed through the hall.

The men at the high table glanced at each other and muttered apologies, obviously with no idea what they were apologising for. What was going on? I turned to Lady Ruth and Lady Margaret. They seemed as bewildered as I was. I looked at Murdoch. Like all the others, he stared at the king.

Macbeth stepped backward, shaking his head. His face was so twisted I hardly knew it. 'Thou canst not say I did it!' he shouted at the empty chair. 'Never shake thy gory locks at me!'

The silence through the hall was thicker than week-old porridge. I wondered we could even breathe.

Lord Ross came to his senses first. 'Gentlemen, rise. His Highness is not well.'

The queen shook her head at him. She drew the king aside, speaking to him urgently. The men at the high table looked uncomfortable, trying to pretend they weren't eavesdropping.

I looked at the raised pie in front of me. Partridge. I could smell the herbs.

Over by the door, the queen whispered reassurance to the king. At last he turned and tried to smile at us — as successfully as a hare might try to fly.

'Eat!' he cried, his voice cracking as it attempted gaiety. 'Do not muse at me, my most worthy friends. I have a strange infirmity, which is nothing to those that know me. Come, love and health to all.' He turned to a servant. 'Give me some wine; fill full!'

The man darted forward with a goblet and a jug. Macbeth held the goblet high.

'I drink to the general joy of the whole table, and to our dear friend Banquo, whom we miss. Would he were here! To all, and him, we thirst, and all to all.'

We stood, the men with their goblets raised. The banners shivered as all shouted out the toast: 'Our duties, and the pledge!'

The moment lengthened as, once again, we waited for the king to sit.

Suddenly he cowered back against the wall. 'Avaunt, and quit my sight!' he shrieked. He raised his arms as if to ward off a blow, muttering words we could not hear.

No silence now. Men muttered. Silk rubbed silk as women whispered. Leather boots scraped on the stones.

The queen moved in front of Macbeth, her long dress partially shielding him from our sight. 'Think of this, good peers, but as a thing of custom. 'Tis no other; only it spoils the pleasure of the time.' I could see the effort she made to keep her voice light.

The king pushed her aside. 'What man dare, I dare!'

He turned and stared again at nothing; or something, perhaps, that none but he could see. 'Approach thou like the rugged Russian bear!' he yelled at his invisible enemy. 'The armed rhinoceros, or the Hyrcan tiger. Take any shape but that, and my firm nerves shall never tremble! Hence, horrible shadow! Unreal mockery, hence!'

And then, just as suddenly, he relaxed. 'Why so, being gone, I am a man again.' His face changed as he noticed us and his lips parted in a ghastly grin. 'Pray you, sit still.'

He had gone mad. No, one couldn't say the king was mad. One could not even think it.

At last he sank into his chair. We sat too. No one spoke, or even dared to catch his neighbour's eye. One of the Highland thanes reached for a slice of salmon, although the king had not yet reached for meat. Most in the hall took his lead and began to eat as well. It was safer to look at salmon and frumenty than each other or the king.

I peered through my eyelashes, trying to look still intent on pike in sorrel sauce. Up at the high table, the queen spoke urgently to the king. At last she took his hand and stood. 'A kind good night to all!' She led him out of the hall.

The silence grew even deeper, as if our chatter had fallen down a well, broken by the sharp looks of the gathered thanes. But tongues would speak daggers tonight. *If he stays bold and resolute*, the queen had told me in the litter. But this king seemed ... I fought the word away, but it came back to me.

The king was mad.

What had made him so? The answer came like an arrow, so swift I could not dodge it. He had heard a witch promise him that he'd be king. I gasped, as if the arrow had been real. The pain felt real too, an agony that spread inside me. What was done could not be undone.

'My dear, are you unwell?' whispered Lady Ruth. 'Come, we must attend the queen.'

I nodded, unable to speak, felt her plump hand take mine.

Macbeth had killed the king, and killed two innocent servants to hide his crime. And his wife had urged him on. But they had not dreamed such a plot until I spoke it.

His guilt was killing him.

His guilt was mine too.

Chapter 12

I saw Lady Ruth grab a pie and hide it in the folds of her skirt as we rose from the table and followed the queen from the hall. It was likely all the food we'd get till supper. We could not leave Her Majesty alone to cope with this.

Lady Ruth handed me a portion of the pie as soon as we were in the corridor. 'Eat,' she said quietly. 'We will have need of it.'

It was lamb's tongue. I tried to nibble it obediently. My tongue had led to this ...

We heard the king still screaming as we climbed the stairs. 'It will have blood, they say. Blood will have blood. Stones have been known to move, and trees to speak!'

We picked up our skirts and tried to hurry without choking, swallowing our pie. I cursed my tight bodice.

Lady Margaret opened the chamber door. The king gaped at us mid-shout.

The queen managed a smile. 'You lack the season of all natures, sleep,' she told her husband in a tone that mimicked calm.

'Yes, we'll to sleep.' He mumbled something more then stumbled out.

I heard the voices of Ross and Lennox outside. They would care for him, thank goodness. How did one tend a mad king?

'My pet, I mean ma'am, you have eaten nothing,' fussed Lady Ruth. 'I will bring a posset and some bread, some minced chicken ...'

'I want nothing.'

'Lambchuck, you must eat.'

Lady Ruth blushed, realising her discourtesy, but the queen just smiled. It wasn't much of a smile, but her eyes were gentle.

'Good Lady Ruth, we thank you for your care. Posset, bread, whatever you think best.'

Lady Ruth bustled out, clearly glad to have something to do. Lady Margaret and I stood helpless. One did not question a queen, even to ask how she was, or what she thought about her husband's sudden madness. We could not even move to take off her banquet gown until she asked.

At last she nodded and held up her arms. We bent to do the unpinning. We had lowered her shift and combed out her hair when Lady Ruth arrived back, servants following her like chicks after a hen, all carrying trays. I glanced at the food, suddenly hungry again despite the hunk of pie. Guilt might crush me, but it hadn't crushed my appetite. Would she bid us eat with her?

She smiled at Lady Ruth as the servants placed the trays on a low table. 'Do you remember how you brought me bread and milk after I ate green apples?' Her voice was light, as if the king screaming like a lunatic was nothing to worry about. 'Now I give thee thanks again. Go back to the feasting hall, kind ladies. You will find company there as well as dinner.'

And be able to reassure everyone that the king had recovered, I thought as I turned to follow the others out.

'Lady Anne.' I turned back. 'I bid you stay.'

'Yes, Your Majesty.'

The door closed and the queen sank onto a cushion. She gestured to me to sit too. I did, glancing hopefully at a dish of chicken and raisins before looking at her. I felt like a puppy asking to be fed.

'Eat,' she said.

'Thank you, ma'am.' I cut a slice of goose and noticed her staring fixedly at the knife. 'May I carve a slice for Your Majesty?'

'No. No, I am quite well with this.' She took a piece of chicken and laid it on her bread, though she didn't lift it to her mouth.

I took it for permission and starting munching. She would talk when she chose.

I tried not to stare at her as I ate. Had this girl really helped to murder a king? Cared so little about the grooms that they could be disposed of as if they were chickens to be plucked? Had it really been cut-throats on the road who had killed Prince Donalbain? And where was Lord Banquo? I realised with growing shock that I had always known what my lady was capable of; had shut my thoughts away as carefully as a fur coat to keep it from the moths.

Food seemed to still my thoughts a little. I had eaten a good helping of goose, a slice of apple pie, and dipped my bread in walnut sauce before the queen spoke again.

'My husband says he saw Lord Banquo's ghost.'

'Is Lord Banquo dead?' I asked carefully.

'If his ghost walks, why then he must be.'

It was a better explanation than 'the king is mad'. Or was it? With growing horror I remembered my words up on the heath. *Thou shalt get kings*, I had promised Banquo. Had my words killed him too?

My hand trembled and I put down my bread. I wondered if I could ever eat again. Or sleep.

'There will be muttering in the corridors tonight,' the queen said. 'It is the worst time for it with half the thanes not yet pledged. Something must be done.' She held my gaze. 'Scotland needs a steady king. There will be disaster otherwise. Civil war, the Danes attacking, perhaps the English too.'

I nodded dumbly. It would be worse than any of King Duncan's wars. And my fault as much as hers.

'We must try the remedy that had such good effect upon the heath at Glamis.' She said the words as casually as if she wanted another loaf of bread.

Another charm? I shuddered. That 'charm' had already caused too much evil. And Agnes was back at Glamis and Mam too.

'Ma'am,' I began.

She cut me off with a stare: a snake mesmerising a mouse to stillness. 'This meat is too large for your village hag. You must hire the actors from England who did perform for us last week. They must pretend to be the witches this time. But now they must reassure the king, not urge him to more action.' She has been thinking of this for days, at least, I thought. One did not plot such an enterprise in an hour, not while trying to soothe the king as well. How long had she suspected he was mad?

And yet I could not do it. *Would* not do it. But it was as if she held me in a hundred skeins of wool. I could not look away.

'You will tell the actors that the play is a simple jest,' she said calmly, as if telling me what petticoats she would wear. 'A play to play with, to frighten your brother-in-law who has not yet pledged to the king. I will make sure the king arrives to see it, in a simple cloak, no crown upon his head. The actors will not realise they are playing for the king himself.'

But the players would recognise him. No, I realised, he hadn't attended the play last week. And this wasn't like at Glamis where all the village knew their thane by sight. Most in the city had never seen the king up close. And these actors were strangers to our city. They would be gone soon too.

'They must add cunning tricks of theatre to make themselves seem truly witch-like. If actors can make us believe they are Caesar and Cleopatra, they can convince a king that they are a tribe of witches, especially as he believes that he met witches before. But the actors must say this.' The queen met my eyes. '*All will be well*. The king is not to worry, not to fret. The kingdom is his, and safe. Let them assure him that no man of woman born can ever kill him. The house of Macbeth shall reign in Scotland,' she smiled, 'till Birnam Wood doth come to Dunsinane.'

I caught my breath. It might work. It *must* work! Something had to be done, or the whole of Scotland would suffer from a mad and trembling king.

If Macbeth, strong in mind after his victory in battle, had trusted what Mam and Agnes and I had told him on the heath, surely now, in his fear and madness, he would believe men whose craft was crafting stories? And he would *want* to believe this, just as he had wanted to believe in our charm.

'He believed that he would be king,' the queen said softly, echoing my thoughts again, 'and so he grasped the throne when it was near. If he believes this, he shall be invincible. And Scotland shall be safe.'

And my guilt would be lessened, just a little.

'They must add one more thing,' said the queen casually. 'The king is not to trust Macduff. That man sees far too much. Can you remember all this?'

'Of course,' I said quietly. 'No man of woman born can ever kill Macbeth. His house is safe till Birnam Wood comes to Dunsinane. And do not trust Macduff. But will the actors do it?'

'Will actors turn down a bag of gold? Of course they will do it. And if the purse is big enough, they will ask no questions.'

The queen stood, and I rose as well. She bent to a chest in the corner, drew out a purse and handed it to me. It was heavy enough to buy our village ten times over.

I was about to ask if Murdoch could come with me, then closed my mouth. No one must know of this. Especially the man to be my husband. But what would happen if the actors gossiped here, or back in England? Or would the queen make sure they did not?

She saw the moment that I understood.

'You must be a shadow dressed in shadows,' she said.

I felt my breath shiver. 'Yes, Your Majesty.'

Chapter 13

I dressed in a black wool gown, put by for mourning, with a black cloth cloak and hood. I didn't have a mask, but fashioned one with a scarf, leaving a slit for my eyes. I pulled it up after I crossed the castle drawbridge and slipped down the track to town, following the lantern lights below me, the pale sweep of roadway. The sea wind moaned softly. A stray cloud slapped fingers of sleet against my eyes. I was glad of the scarf.

I'd never been as cold as this, even in the weeks before Agnes took us starved and freezing to her cottage. My bones, my heart, were cold. I tried to mouth a prayer. It would not come. One wrong had led to other wrongs. Now I was doing wrong again, even if it was to try to make the first wrong right. This was sin, and I was part of it.

And yet the king was still the king and my mistress still the queen. A loyal subject does the bidding of Their Majesties. Surely it was better that Scotland had a strong king, confident to rule, and not one shivering at shadows?

And if Macbeth had killed Duncan? Well, Duncan had killed men too; not by his own hand perhaps, but by his years of senseless battles, sending others to kill in his name. Men like my da, who'd been killed in turn. Did all kings have so much blood upon their hands?

But to kill the grooms! Men like me, who only did their duty.

I had done far more than my duty, and it had led to this.

Had Macbeth killed Prince Donalbain too, and Lord Banquo? Had he truly seen Banquo's ghost at the banquet, or was it his own conscience that had terrified him?

The first cottages belonged to those who worked for the castle: neat and well thatched, with gardens of cabbages, turnips and sea kale. Merchants' homes next, on the heights where they could watch to see their ships sail in or out, above the stink of the town proper. Candle and lamp light flickered in halls or kitchens. The streets were as deserted as the village tracks in a blizzard.

Houses dwindled into shacks, then huddled to become a town. I lifted my skirts above a cobbled mess of rotting cabbage leaves mixed with the mess of chamber pots and horses. Respectable houses had their lights out by now. But this was the haunt of tavern folk and actors; lanterns swung dread shadows across the road in the wind from the sea.

I peered up at the tavern signs: a pair of cockerels; an ape and horse; a dragon and thistle. None were the ones I was hunting.

A pair of apprentices appeared out of a nearby inn. 'What ho, a bawd!' one called. 'Pretty lady, I'll give to thee a penny.'

His companion reached into his breeches. 'Nay, I have something more for you than copper.'

'Pray, good men,' I said hurriedly, 'I am looking for The Two Roosters, the actors' tavern.'

'Ha! She wants roosters! We'll give you more rollicking than four and twenty actors!'

'Sirs, I am their wife,' I said desperately, then realised I'd implied I was married to the whole company.

But they missed my slip. One bowed, his cap sweeping the ground. 'Apologies, gentle lady.' He indicated the tavern they'd just left. 'This is The Two Roosters.' The sign swung above us, too faded to make out in the erratic light. 'You will find your actors on the second floor, discussing their small parts.'

'Small parts,' giggled the other youth.

His friend nudged him. 'Sirrah, she is respectable.'

The first youth shrugged. 'She married an actor — she must be used to worse. Ma'am, I kiss your dirty shoe.'

One good punch for each, I thought, in the place where Agnes said men were vulnerable. But it would only make a fuss. I scurried past them instead, and they bowed, their own small parts still safe.

The Two Roosters smelled of sour ale and sourer feet. The stairs creaked as I stepped up them. There was but one room above, the floor made of mouse droppings as much as wood. It held a battered table lit by tallow candles, with three men and a boy in tattered finery sitting around it on the floor. They stared at me, and came to the same conclusion as the youths outside.

'An angel come to pleasure us!' One of the men stood and bowed, as courtly as a thane. He had silver hair and was clean-shaven, although his hose were patched. 'Richard Burbage of Lord Knudson's Men at your service, gentle lady. And this be William Kempe, and John Heminges, and this brat be Robert Goughe. Our purses are sadly light, for the good fellows of this town are niggardly in coin as well as praise and understanding. And yet you are most welcome to share our cheese and,' he squinted at the table, 'and what might, by some, be called bread.'

'I haven't come for bread,' I said. I pulled out the pouch, half full now of what the queen had given me. They gaped at it; gaped more when I said, 'Gold.'

'In truth an angel,' said young Robert. 'That purse would buy each of us a small estate —'

Master Burbage kicked him. 'Quiet.' His faded but keen eyes stared at me, all mockery gone. 'What is my lady's pleasure?'

I took a breath, then wished I hadn't as my nose filled with the stink of aged tallow and even older cheese. 'My ... husband wishes to trick his brother, a thane who has not yet pledged allegiance to the king.'

'They say the king is mad,' said William Kempe.

'And those that say it may be hanged for treason.' Burbage's voice had an edge. 'Lady, we are not of this land, but while we are, we are loyal to its king. What trick is this?'

He didn't believe me. He would, however, believe in the pouch. I opened it, and heard their breaths draw in at the sight of all that gold.

'And another, equal to this, when you have played your parts,' I said.

'And what is the play?' asked Master Burbage quietly.

'No play, or only part of one. You must be hags and prophesy to convince my husband's brother that no man of woman born can kill the king, and that Macbeth's house shall stand till Birnam Wood shall come to Dunsinane.'

'You want us to play witches!' cried young Robert excitedly.

'For a small time only, and for an audience of one, or maybe two. Can ... can you make my brother-in-law believe that you are magic?'

'Of course!' Robert turned to the others eagerly. 'We can use the trick with flour to make fog, and William can do the lanterns —'

'Silence.' Burbage quelled him with another glance. He looked at me. 'Lady, I have no liking to play witchcraft. I have even less wish to meddle in loyalties to kings.'

I held up the pouch of gold.

He looked at it, then around the room, taking in the tallow candles and the cheese rind on the table. He sighed. 'Judas played his part for thirty pieces of silver. At least we do this for gold. It shall be done, exactly as you wish.' No flourishes now and, for the first time, sincerity.

'You think he will believe it?'

Burbage gave a grim smile. 'For that much gold, and at this time, I would convince the rolling sea that it was a bowl of soup. The skills we have are yours, lady. And they are enough.'

I believed him, far more than if he'd boasted. 'Good. Where should it be done?'

They knew a cave. How, I did not know. I supposed men who travelled for their living must have ways of knowing such things. I did not ask them, and they did not ask any more questions of me — not my name, nor even the name of my brother-in-law. Gold bought discretion.

I sat and listened while they discussed the words, the tricks to make them real. I knew little of the theatre, but they knew their craft. They called for new candles twice before the play was set.

Finally Burbage glanced out the window, where dawn's light was appearing. 'It is done. Lady, hie you hence and to your bed.'

I did not tell him that my bed was usually in the queen's chamber, or that dawn made a mockery of any sleep I'd hoped to have. But perhaps Her Majesty would give me leave to slip away to sleep after we'd dressed her. I would need it if I was to stay awake to watch the king tonight.

But would it be tonight? I realised I didn't know.

I stood, trying not to sway. 'I will send word when you are to perform. It will be soon. And now, good night.'

'Good day rather,' said Burbage kindly. 'And good it was that sent you to us.' He hesitated, then met my eyes. 'This is the king we play for, is it not?'

I bit my lips, then nodded. These men deserved the truth.

'There is only one who would have easy access to so much gold as you have given us tonight,' said Burbage quietly. 'Nay, you need not tell us her name. But from your speech and manner I judge you to be gentle not just of birth but also of temper. How did you get coiled in this?'

Tears stung my eyes. 'I ... I cannot say.'

'Is there no home you can go to away from such trickeries and lies? Do not worry,' Burbage added quickly, 'we will do your bidding.' His smile grew wry. 'And get our second purse. But doings such as this are not fit for such as you.'

'I must do what I must,' I said. 'Out of duty and loyalty.'

And guilt, my mind whispered. All this had come from those words I'd uttered on the heath. Lord Banquo was dead because I'd said his children would be kings. Macbeth had murdered him so he could not sire more. Did that mean Banquo's son, Fleance, was killed as well? How many more were still to die because a foolish girl had ordered a charm and another foolish girl had given more than she'd been asked for, both of us drunk with a force we did not understand?

Agnes was right. Words had power. Words could wield swords, and death, and kings.

I looked at Burbage. He was a kind man, concerned for me and risking so much for the security of his players. I glanced at young Robert, chewing at the wax that had covered the cheese; and at William Kempe and John Heminges, discussing together how they might heighten the effects of the play they had so skilfully crafted for me. I liked them all.

'Master Burbage,' I said carefully, 'there is one final thing. I ... I think it best, when you have done this thing, that you should all vanish.'

'Why, yes, that is how we agreed it would go. The lights shall be blown out and it will seem as if the darkness swallows us.'

'Not just in the play. In ... in truth too.' I swallowed.

'After the play, can you vanish from this town as surely as you will vanish in the cave?'

Burbage met my eyes. I saw that he understood.

'If we can vanish once, then we can do it twice.' He smiled, an actor's smile that did not reach his eyes. 'Actors are well practised at vanishing. A tavern bill unpaid, a lover promised even though the actor be already wed. And with a pouch of gold to ease our way, Scotland shall not see us more.'

'Where will you go?' I asked.

The actor's smile again. 'Away.'

I nodded. It was best. As Agnes always said, closed mouths caught no flies. I could not let slip what I did not know.

He hesitated, then added, 'Lady, you could come with us. A wig, a boy's clothes and a youth's beard stuck to your chin — no one would know you. We could take you safe to your family, or to my sister's house if there are none to take you in.'

The tears threatened to come again. 'You ... you are most kind. But I must stay.'

'I offer only what I hope a man in my place would do for my own daughter,' he said gently. 'If you change your mind, you have just to let us know.'

'Thank you. But I won't.'

I wished so deeply that I could.

Chapter 14

Thunder crashed and rolled. Not a real storm, but a drum, cunningly wielded by Richard Heminges in the darkness of the cave. I stood beside him, my face darkened again with soot, my body shrouded by my cloak and scarf, and peered towards the cave's entrance.

The queen had planned to tell the king today that she'd had a dream: the long grand host of Scottish kings had waved the banner of Clan Macbeth, and shouted out his name; she had also seen this cave, and seen him striding from it, his face wreathed in deepest joy.

But they would have no private time together till after midday dinner, and by then I had to be with the actors here, ensuring all was ready.

What if an urgent messenger had come, and she'd had no time alone with him? What if he had not believed her, had laughed, and said it was no more than a woman's fancy?

No. When the queen spoke these days, the king obeyed.

But what if he said, 'It must be tomorrow. I have already agreed to drink with the ambassador from Denmark tonight'? What if instead of coming alone, he brought guards? The actors could fool one man, or several. But a troop of guards? And some guards, at least, would gossip. A king who conspired with witches was worse than one who was mad.

The moments flickered by. I wished a kirk was near, so that we could hear the hour struck, and know the time. Time seemed to have vanished in this cave, or rather, each tiny part seemed stretched into a day. But doings such as these seemed too wrong to play out below the kind glance of a kirk.

Master Burbage glanced at me, though it was hard to recognise him, dressed in black rags, his face thick with white lead and stuck about with pustules of squashed raspberry. A long nose, a wig of horsehair plaited with straw. No one would ever have taken this crone for Richard Burbage, actor. He had received his second purse of gold. He had trusted me, as he trusted his company to do this right. But I no longer knew if it was right or not.

'I think we must begin,' he whispered.

'But the ... our audience is not here yet.'

Burbage shook his head. 'A play begins when the audience arrives. But if ... our audience ... is to believe that this is no play tonight, but real, it must seem as if he arrives while we go about our business.'

My head felt full of wool from weariness. 'But he might miss the most important part!' We had laboured so long to make every word and scene count.

'Trust me,' said Burbage quietly. 'We have put in another scene. If the ... audience ... sees it, it will build his awe. If he does not, it helps to build our own.' He smiled slightly. I saw two of his strong white teeth had been blackened.

He clicked his fingers. It must have been a signal, for a single light flickered. It seemed to float just below his chin, illuminating only his face.

'Why, how now, Hecate!' the crone who had been Richard Burbage screeched.

Another flash of light. Even though I knew it was black powder and a tinder, I almost screamed. A younger, powerful woman appeared, her face with a masculine beauty. William Kempe, I thought.

'Have I not reason, beldams as you are,' 'Hecate' cried, 'saucy and overbold? How did you dare to trade and traffic with Macbeth in riddles and affairs of death; and I, the mistress of your charms, the close contriver of all harms, was never called to bear my part, or show the glory of our art?'

This looked like witchcraft. None could call it else. I had not agreed to this!

But the play was begun now. Had begun when I had said those words upon the moor. To stop it now would mean disaster, my queen's fury; dismissal from her service at best.

But I would not listen. I tried instead to remember one of the songs Murdoch had sung to me. How did it go? *A rose will bloom among the snow, and I the only one to know ...*

I started as different music swept across the cave, a strange wailing of the pipes, played out of tune. Hecate vanished; or at least the light that showed her was covered by a sack. Only three figures danced now: the hag; a girl who had the look of young Rob, despite her greasy locks and blackened teeth and lips as red as blood; and a woman, white-faced as Burbage's hag but with blood that dripped down from her eyes. I knew the red was wine lees, but felt chilled even so. There was evil in this cave tonight, but not wrought by the actors. Evil had spread across the land ever since I'd unleashed Macbeth's ambition.

The music stopped. Light gleamed on a cauldron to one side. Round about it the three figures circled.

'Thrice the brinded cat hath mewed,' cackled Burbage's hag.

'Thrice and once the hedge-pig whined,' muttered Heminges's white-faced woman.

Young Rob screamed, 'Harper cries, "'Tis time, 'tis time!"'

But it isn't time yet, I thought despairingly. Where was Macbeth? Must the actors sing and dance all night, in case he came? How long could they keep up their play? The queen and I should have worked out a signal, to show that he was near — but that would have meant trusting someone else.

The hag sang, her voice cracked and terrible:

'Round about the cauldron go;
In the poisoned entrails throw.
Toad, that under cold stone
Days and nights has thirty-one
Sweltered venom sleeping got,
Boil thou first in the charmed pot.'

They all joined in:

'Double, double toil and trouble;
Fire burn and cauldron bubble.'

'Fillet of a fenny snake!' shrieked the white-faced woman.

'In the cauldron boil and bake;
Eye of newt and toe of frog ...'

I thought of Agnes's snail broth, and the snakes she sometimes added, and yes, frogs too. Could she be made to seem like a witch to those who did not know her? Every fibre of me wished to call out, 'Stop! This isn't right! Let all men be moved by good, not evil, including kings.' But I was a thread in the tapestry of state, just like Da had been, marching to another's orders to another's war, both of us carried where the king and queen decided we must be stitched.

'... *Wool of bat and tongue of dog,*' the player screeched.

'*Adder's fork and blind-worm's sting,*

Lizard's leg and owlet's wing,

For a charm of powerful trouble,

Like a hell-broth boil and bubble.'

The three joined hands about the cauldron and sang together:

'*Double, double toil and trouble;*

Fire burn and cauldron bubble.'

'*Scale of dragon, tooth of wolf,*' sang young Robert, in a whisper that echoed through the cave.

A true actor, I thought, admiring despite my fear and horror. Where was the king? I almost hoped he would not come. None could blame the actors then, nor blame me ...

'*Witches' mummy, maw and gulf*

Of the ravined salt-sea shark,' continued Robert.

'*Root of hemlock digged in the dark,*

Liver of blaspheming Jew,

Gall of goat, and slips of yew

Slivered in the moon's eclipse,

Nose of Turk and Tartar's lips,

Finger of birth-strangled babe

Ditch-delivered by a drab,

Make the gruel thick and slab.

Add thereto a tiger's chaudron,

For the ingredients of our cauldron.'

The three witches joined hands again, and sang together:

'Double, double toil and trouble;
Fire burn and cauldron bubble.'

A horse whinnied outside the cave. The white-faced woman held up her hands. 'By the pricking of my thumbs, something wicked this way comes,' she cried. The sound echoed weirdly. 'Open, locks, whoever knocks!'

For a moment I thought I would faint. I leaned back against the slimy cave wall. Lights flashed as one of the actors swiftly pulled the sacks off the lanterns. The thunder drum rumbled again — and there stood the king, alone and amazed. How much had he heard?

'How now, you secret, black, and midnight hags?' His voice trembled. He had thought to see kings here, not witches. 'What is it you do?'

The actors stared at him, then chorused in one hiss: 'A deed without a name.'

Macbeth straightened. Suddenly I saw the warrior again. His voice rang as hard as steel. 'I conjure you, by that which you profess — however you come to know it — answer me. Though you untie the winds and let them fight, though castles topple on their warders' heads, even till destruction sicken, answer me to what I ask you.'

Burbage's hag peered at him through the gloom. 'Speak!' she hissed.

'Demand!' sang the white-faced woman with her bleeding eyes.

'We'll answer,' announced young Robert, leering at the king.

'Would you rather hear it from our mouths, or from our masters?' demanded the hag.

Macbeth put his hands upon his hips, defiant. 'Call them. Let me see them.'

The hag nodded as if she had expected that answer, which of course Burbage had.

'Pour in sow's blood that hath eaten her nine farrow,' he muttered over the cauldron. 'Grease that's sweaten from the murderer's gibbet throw into the flame.'

'Come, high or low,' they all chanted. 'Thyself and office deftly show!'

The lights vanished. For three heartbeats the dark sat heavy as a grinding stone, then a single light flashed deep inside the cave. A bodiless head with a bloody neck appeared to float there. I almost screamed, even though I knew it was Richard in a dark cloak, the light shining only on his head and neck.

Macbeth stepped forward. 'Tell me, thou unknown power —'

Burbage's hag wagged a grimy finger at him. 'He knows thy thought. Hear his speech, but say thou nought.'

The bloodied head spoke: 'Macbeth! Macbeth! Macbeth! *Beware Macduff. Beware the Thane of Fife.* Dismiss me. Enough.'

The light was covered and the head vanished.

Macbeth nodded. 'Whatever thou art, for thy good caution, thanks. Thou hast harped my fear aright. But one word more —'

The hag cackled again. 'He will not be commanded. Here's another more potent than the first.'

The thunder boomed beside me, so loudly I put my hands to my ears.

Darkness swept the cave once more. Something fluttered past my head. I thought it another illusion, then realised it was a bat, startled by our noise.

A light flickered and a baby girl appeared, her blonde hair matted with blood, blood smeared upon her face and clothes. I had to blink to see her, and knew Macbeth would too, for clear sight would have shown she was just a doll.

'Macbeth! Macbeth! Macbeth!' the girl whispered.

The king stepped forward. 'Had I three ears, I'd hear thee.'

'Be bloody, bold, and resolute.' Her words seemed to flicker with her image. 'Laugh to scorn the power of man, *for none of woman born shall harm Macbeth.*'

The girl doll vanished and I gripped my hands together

so hard my fingers hurt. Two prophecies done. Now for the last ...

The king smiled. I shrank to see it. This was not just a warrior, but the man who had slain Duncan. Yes, Duncan had been a poor king, but that did not make it right. And then death upon death to cover up that first shame.

'Then live, Macduff,' Macbeth muttered. 'What need I fear of thee? But yet I'll make assurance double sure, and take a bond of fate. Thou shalt not live, that I may sleep in spite of thunder.'

My skin turned colder than the cave. Now he planned to kill Macduff too. How many must be sacrificed before the king felt he was safe?

The thunder boomed again. Another light flickered to my right. Another doll, this time a boy, with a silver paper crown upon his head and a branch propped up in his hand.

Macbeth peered into the darkness, trying to make the figure out. 'What is this that rises like the issue of a king, and wears upon his baby-brow the round and top of sovereignty?'

The actors hissed together from the darkness: 'Listen, but speak not to it.'

The boy spoke. His voice made me shudder, though I knew it was but William further back in the darkness. 'Be lion-mettled, proud; and take no care who chafes, who frets, or where conspirers are. *Macbeth shall never vanquished be until Great Birnam Wood to high Dunsinane Hill shall come against him.*'

The flickering light was covered and I heard Macbeth's voice in the shadows, gloating and confident now.

'That will never be! Who can impress the forest, bid the tree unfix his earth-bound root? Good! Yet my heart throbs to know one thing.' His voice rose as he yelled into the cave's darkness, 'Tell me, if your art can tell so much: shall Banquo's issue ever reign in this kingdom?'

I held my breath. We hadn't rehearsed an answer for this question. I hadn't even told the actors about Banquo. What could they say?

'Seek to know no more!' their voices chorused in the gloom.

Macbeth strode forward. 'I will be satisfied!' he yelled. 'Deny me this, and an eternal curse fall on you! Let me know.'

Another few steps and he'd find the lamps and the drum. And me.

He halted suddenly as a light gleamed dimly to one side. I tried to breathe again.

'Why sinks that cauldron?' he demanded. 'And what noise is this?'

'Show!' yelled Burbage in the blackness. I supposed he was giving himself time to work out an answer.

'Show!' screamed the white-faced woman.

'Show!' shrieked young Robert.

'Show his eyes, and grieve his heart,' they chorused. 'Come like shadows, so depart!'

Another light flared. Suddenly a shadow appeared on the cave wall, a crown upon its head. Two heartbeats and it was gone. Another shadow of a crown followed it, and then another.

I felt as if my heart must stop. Were these truly kingly visions?

Then I caught a hint of movement: Robert, walking past the lantern to cast a shadow on the wall behind. Yes, these actors knew their craft.

Or did they? For, as the eighth shadow passed, the king cried out, 'Thou art too like the spirit of Banquo. Down! Thy crown does sear mine eyeballs. Filthy hags! Why do you show me this? The blood-boltered Banquo smiles upon me!'

The hag's face appeared. 'Ay, sir, all this is so. But why stands Macbeth thus amazedly?' Burbage's tone turned reassuring:

'Come, sisters, cheer we up his sprites,
And show the best of our delights:
I'll charm the air to give a sound,
While you perform your antic round.
That this great king may kindly say,
Our duties did his welcome pay.'

More lights flashed. The pipes played, in tune now. The three danced, hand in hand. And then the lamps went out. No light. No sound, except another bat speeding for the cleaner and quieter air outside.

The king strode forward. 'Where are they? Gone? Let this pernicious hour stand aye accursed in the calendar!' He turned towards a movement at the mouth of the cave. 'Come in, without there!'

'Your Majesty?' said a male voice. I recognised it as the Earl of Lennox's. He must have just arrived. 'I saw your horse outside. What is Your Grace's will?'

'Saw you the weird sisters?' the king demanded.

'No, my lord.' Lennox seemed puzzled, not just at the question, but at finding his king inside a dark and dripping cave.

'Came they not by you?' Macbeth's voice was almost a shriek.

'No, indeed, my lord,' said Lennox, startled.

'Infected be the air whereon they ride,' Macbeth snarled. 'And damned all those that trust them! I did hear the galloping of horse. Who was it came by?'

''Tis two or three messengers, my lord, to bring you word. Macduff is fled to England.'

The queen was right, I thought. Macduff must have sniffed out Macbeth's treachery and gone to join Malcolm.

I stood there shivering, from fright as much as cold. The actors knew now that they'd played not just for the king, but for a man who'd as good as admitted to murder, and would murder Macduff if he could. They were good men, despite the play of witchcraft here. Could they escape the queen's reach? Or would their bodies be added to the pyre of King Duncan, Prince Donalbain, and the grooms? If they escaped, would they keep the secret?

Something dripped on my neck. I bit off a cry. Just water from the roof. If I screamed once, I knew I would not stop.

At last I heard footfalls as the king and Lord Lennox left the cave. I listened still, unmoving, until there came the sound of horses speeding away into the night.

'Master Burbage?' I whispered.

No answer.

I spoke louder. 'Master Kempe? Robert?'

Another drip fell into the silence.

I pulled off the cloak that had blanketed my own lamp, and held it up. The cave walls gleamed damp and empty.

The actors had gone.

Chapter 15

The porter winked at me as I slipped through the palace gate. He took me for a servant in my plain cloth cloak, gone to meet a lover.

'A good night, lass?' he asked.

'Yes, thank you, sir.' I let my voice drift back to the accent of the village and handed him a penny.

He smirked and tapped his breeches. 'I have a good knight here if ye be lonely.'

'Cook will be looking for me to light the fires soon, sir.'

'Well, if you feel like a stronger broth than any in the kitchen, you come to me.' He winked again.

I nodded as if I hadn't understood, and ran across the courtyard then up the servants' stairs. No torches in the sconces here that might show who I was; nor were there any guards in the corridor outside the queen's chamber.

I scratched on her door and entered, then halted. The king lay in the bed, naked and asleep.

The queen lifted her finger to her lips, then slipped silently from the covers. I followed her into the robing room.

'It went well,' she murmured. 'He is come back resolute as a tiger. He laughed for the first time since the crown weighted so his brow. Even his steps conquered the stones of Dunsinane. And no one else saw?'

I shook my head. 'The Earl of Lennox and his men arrived after the ... hags had vanished, Your Majesty.'

'The actors suspected nothing?'

I shook my head. 'No, ma'am.' It was the first time I had lied to her. Would she see it?

She smiled.

If a tiger smiled, it would be like that, I thought. She was well matched with her husband. Macbeth had been a good man once: loyal to his kin, content with Glamis. She had made him king; perhaps now she could make him a good one. Good for the land; confident enough to stare down rebellion before it came to arms, not pitching battles like apprentices pitched horseshoes.

The queen watched me. I hoped my thoughts did not show on my face.

'The actors left?' she asked.

'Yes, ma'am.'

'Did they say where they were bound?'

Her voice was casual, but my body froze.

I forced a smile. 'Only that it would be far and fast, and that they would not speak.'

She stood silent in her bare feet and her shift. At last she nodded. 'If they do speak, they condemn themselves for practising at witchcraft. Yes, they will be silent.'

Was that threat a sword point for me too? A warning that if I whispered any of this, even to Murdoch or the queen's other women, I would condemn myself?

I met her eyes and for the second time that night spoke in my real voice, the accent of my village. 'I am loyal.'

Another smile, a true one now. At least I thought it true.

'I know.' She looked at me consideringly. 'I will suggest to the king tomorrow that Lord Murdoch should be made commander of our guard, to replace the traitor Banquo. Should you care to be married on Midsummer's Eve?'

I understood. My reward for this night's work was the highest estate possible for my husband. But I must also be sent to Greymouth, far from court, where most of the year my husband would be far from me and any tales I might tell.

'I thank Your Majesty,' I said formally.

'I will miss you,' she said, her voice soft. 'When your children are old enough to learn to wield a sword, you must come to court again. We shall be old women together, sharing whispers before the fire.'

She put out her hand and took mine, then leaned and kissed my cheek. It was the first time she had ever touched me; always until now I had been the servant, tending her.

'Live well and happily, Annie,' she whispered.

'I ... I hope I will, Your Majesty.'

The king himself announced at dinner the next day that Murdoch and I would be wed. The king stood straight today, his voice firm, his eyes clear as if he saw no ghosts lingering in the hall — or as if the ones he saw were kind. I almost forgave myself the part I had played to give him strength again, though my conscience nibbled, rat-like, through the feast.

It should have been the proudest moment of my life, the whole court cheering Annie Grasseyes, and with affection too. I had made friends here. Friends who did not know the trickery below my smile, my secret service to the queen. Probably, used to court intrigues, they would think there was nothing to forgive. But I could not forgive myself. For all my brocade dress and jewels, this was not who I wished to be.

Lord Murdoch gave me a golden ring: made by the goldsmith just for me, and showing two seals joined, the emblem of his house. It gleamed upon my finger as I tended my mistress, or sewed the tapestry chair covers I would take to Greymouth Manor as part of my dowry. I wore the ring always, not keeping it in the box where I stored my other precious things: the ruby necklace, the silver brooch, a thick gold chain like woven wheat to wear about my waist, given me by the queen, a lock of Mam's hair, Rab's cloak pin and his letters. They still came each week, and each week I kept the slip of paper in my bodice, next to my body, until the scent of home was gone.

But I would have a new home soon. I had gripped my courage in both hands and asked Murdoch if Mam could come with me as nurse.

He'd looked surprised, then bowed and kissed my hand, and then my wrist. 'Of course, my lady. I am your servant in this, as in all matters.'

I couldn't tell if the surprise came from my obvious fear he might say no; or if he'd forgotten I came from humble stock, my estate newly granted by the lady wife of Cawdor, and made larger when she had become queen. I noted he did not add, 'Your mother must come here for our wedding.'

I still hadn't written to tell Mam of my marriage. I would not have the minister of the kirk read it to her, nor Rab. It would be best, I decided, to send a messenger when it was done, along with some grand gifts that would show my new estate to all the village before Mam left it to be with me at Greymouth. A fur cloak and cobbled shoes, and what would seem part of the wedding feast — pies and candied fruits and a roast goose. Let Mam think the wedding had been so quickly done that I couldn't send word to her.

Could I ever confess the scene in the cave to Mam? Tell her that I'd served a king and queen who murdered enemies? Mam had raised me to do good. So had Agnes, in her way.

And what of Agnes, after I was wed? I would offer her a home at Greymouth, but I was sure she would not come. If I couldn't see her in an earl's household, I doubted she would either. But I would arrange with Glamis's steward for a young man to be sent regularly to keep the cottage sound and the peat piled up, and a haunch of mutton every week, cheese and bags of oats and flour. I — no, my steward, for I'd soon have one too — could hire a village girl to tend her each day and in the night too as she grew frail, to make her pots of soup. Though no one's soup was as good as Agnes's own.

'Lady Anne?' Lady Margaret peered at me from the doorway to the queen's chamber. 'You seem far away.'

'What?' I remembered myself — ladies did not say 'what' — and added, 'My apologies. My mind wandered.' I sought a suitable place for it to wander to. 'I was thinking of the king as he visits the Highland thanes.'

The king had ridden off, as he should have months before, with just a small retinue of men, partly for speed, but more importantly because a small party on horseback said, 'I need no army at my back to ensure Scotland's loyalty.'

Lady Margaret smiled approvingly. 'The queen has asked for you. She would to bed.'

'Of course. I come.' I put down my tapestry.

The queen hadn't called for me to dress her since the night I'd reported on the actors' performance in the cave. She had, smiling, made the excuse that I would have much to occupy me before my wedding, but in truth there'd been little to do beyond agreeing with the steward about the foods for the wedding banquet, and embroidering the chair covers, a task Lady Margaret had informed me that every bride should do. If there was any other preparation needed to please a husband, she did not tell me of it.

I tried to imagine myself at the head of the table as my guests sat on the new chair covers. I would wear the keys of the manor house at my waist; give orders to the steward and my servants. A fine vision, but I couldn't see it, no matter how hard I tried.

The queen was already in her shift, leaning back against the cushions of her bed. An apple-wood fire snickered in the hearth.

She held out her hands to me. 'Lady Anne, I have missed you.'

I took her hands and curtseyed at the same time, then leaned forward as she showed that she would kiss my cheek.

She nodded to Lady Margaret and Lady Ruth. 'Thank you, good ladies.' As their skirts whispered through the doorway, the queen gestured to the truckle bed. 'Stay. Talk to me.'

'What of, Your Majesty?'

'Happy things. I ... I have had dreams again since the king left to make his progress round the land. Harsh dreams. Perchance if you talk of sweetness, my dreams will turn sweet too.'

'Agnes, the old woman I lived with before I came to the castle, said that eating quince before bed gives a person nightmares.' I didn't add that she recommended snail broth instead.

The queen attempted a smile. 'I have eaten no quince.'

She looked tired, as if the sleep she had managed did not refresh her. I tried to think of happy things. Babies gave joy, but she had lost hers and there was no sign of another yet. Weddings, perhaps? But in truth, the road to mine was not the unclouded journey that I'd hoped.

'I could tell you about Mistress Farthing's gander, ma'am.'

Her smile was almost genuine now. 'What about the gander?'

'Oh, it was a fine one, the biggest in the village. Mistress Farthing was as proud of that gander as a captain of his ship. One day her husband sold a mob of sheep to the castle and got a gold coin for them. None in the village had ever seen such a thing, nor was he backward in showing it around. He showed that gold coin at the smithy, and after kirk, and to his friends upon the green as they sat drinking their ale. And that was where he dropped it, onto the grass. Quicker than lightning, the gander swallowed it.

'"Give me my coin, ye feathered fool!" old Farthing cried. "Wife, get my axe!"

'"You'll not be chopping up my gander!" she yelled back.

'"But, wife, my coin!"

'"A gander's not a goose," she said. "It lays no golden eggs. The coin will be safe inside its gizzard. Safer, perhaps, for my gander isn't fool enough to show it off."'

The queen laughed. 'What happened then?'

'Old Farthing did his wife's bidding of course. What man wants a cold bed and cold porridge? But he didn't let that gander out of his sight. He followed it around everywhere, like a puppy after its mam.'

'I think I know what happened,' she said. 'A dog ate the gander? A wolf?'

I grinned. 'No, ma'am. It fell in love! Not with any of the Farthings' flock, nor any of the geese in the village. This was a wild goose, swimming in the river while the flock was grazing on its banks. I know for I was there, watching our goat, and there was this fine white goose, floating like a swan. The gander flapped his wings and flew to join her. And that was the last we saw of them and the gold coin too — two geese a-swimming down the burn, and old Farthing running after them, yelling, "Give me my coin, ye varmint! Give me back my coin!"'

The queen laughed again and settled back on her pillows. 'A good story. A gold coin for a goose's dowry. We must dower you with gold as well as land. I will see to it.' Her eyes were closing. 'Sleep in the truckle bed tonight,' she whispered. 'You can guard me from my dreams again.'

'Most willingly, ma'am.'

I slipped into the robing room and took off my gown and slippers, then crept back to the truckle bed in my shift. She was already asleep.

A cry woke me. I had been dreaming of wild geese, and for a moment thought it was their call. Then I saw the queen had vanished.

I ran to the door in time to see her, still barefoot and in her shift, drifting down the corridor. Should I call to her? But if she wished to be private ...

I tried to think. Surely she had not taken a lover with the king away? And if she had, would it not be much safer for him to come to her? And why ask me to sleep in the truckle bed? Besides, her look was ... strange.

I crept after her, the stones cold under my feet, even so far into summer. She floated up the stairs, so quiet in her white shift she could almost be a ghost. Up another set of stairs, and then another, till she came to the small door that led to the battlements.

I followed her to the edge of the palace wall. For a moment I was afraid she might fall, but she stood still, gazing across the sleeping city and the hills and heath beyond.

'Blood,' she whispered, 'blood across the land. Blood calls to blood, whispered from shattered veins. Blood calls vengeance to the blood that shed it ...' She looked down at her hands, small and white in the blue starlight. 'Will these hands never be clean?' She wiped them against her night shift. 'There! A spot! And there another!'

She gazed at her hands again, then began to rub them frenziedly against the stones. She would rub them raw!

I ran to her. 'Ma'am, come. I'll wash your hands.'

She looked, but did not see me. But at least the desperate movement ceased.

'Once there was a wife of Cawdor, now no wife nor lady any more,' she muttered piteously. 'What has become of her?'

I didn't know if the rebel thane's wife was even still alive. What did happen to the widows of rebel lords? I knew too bitterly that few people noticed widows like my mam, or cared.

'Ma'am, come downstairs. Come, sleep,' I murmured, as if she were a child. Even though I knew she was asleep,

I hesitated to put my hands on her. You did not touch a queen unasked.

'Sleep,' she whispered. 'Macbeth hath murdered sleep. Banquo's son, Macduff's puppies and their dam, all slain. Their blood ... their blood ...'

I gazed at her in horror. Banquo's son dead too? And Macduff's children? No wonder her conscience screamed at night.

My own conscience whimpered like a kitten drowning in a sack. How much of this was due to me? But I must care for the queen now.

I forced myself to breathe slowly and deeply. *Calm your body and you calm your mind*, Agnes had said the night a blizzard crouched and sucked about the village and we feared we'd lose the cottage roof before the dawn.

If Scotland was to have peace, its heads of state must be calm and rational. And if my part in that was to reassure the queen, that was what I must do.

Before I could move, the queen stared at her hands again. 'I must wash,' she muttered. 'I must wash and wash.' To my relief she drifted back towards the stairs.

I followed her to her room, and lay awake long after she had fallen asleep again. Who could I go to for help? I could not speak about the queen sleepwalking and crying out her sins, not even to Lady Ruth and Lady Margaret, loyal as they were. Not now I knew the cause.

Had she given the order for Banquo's son and Macduff's wife and children to be slain? Or had it been the king? I could not ask.

The next night she walked again. There was only one person in the palace who might help me now. I had to tell the doctor.

Chapter 16

Once more the queen had me wait on her after Lady Ruth and Lady Margaret had prepared her for bed. Once more I told her a story, this time of the kitten that hid in the cauldron and yowled when Agnes poured the water in, then stalked over to the hearth, curled up there and staked it as hers forever, and Agnes as her servant.

At last the queen slept. I slipped a dress over my shift, then pulled on stockings, slippers and a cloak. I hesitated, then hung the queen's cloak on the doorknob.

The doctor waited outside her chamber. He would not be fond of me if I had called him out of his bed for nothing. He was a grand man who wore black velvet, and gold rings upon his fingers. But he had served three kings and whispered nothing. If there was anyone in the castle I could trust, it was him.

I waited too. The bell tolled ten, eleven, midnight. Still the queen did not stir.

And then, suddenly, she rose. Silent as the castle graveyard, she unlocked her closet and took out paper. She wrote upon it, her fingers holding a quill that wasn't there. What was she writing? I could read far better now, but couldn't follow the quickness of her fingers as she made the letters. She folded the paper, picked up a seal as incorporeal as the quill, stamped it and set it down.

I watched as she slipped back to bed. Was this all she would do tonight, and the doctor not here to see it? But she didn't lie down. Instead she looked at her fingers, rubbed them hard against her shift, then almost ran towards the door. Her fingers met the cloak. As I'd hoped, she draped it around her shoulders as she drifted out.

The doctor pressed back against the wall as she passed him, bowing low. She didn't see him. He met my eyes, nodded silently, and we hurried after her.

Up the stairs, around, around, her bare feet making no noise. The doctor's boots clattered on the stone, but she did not hear. And then the battlements.

The moon sailed tonight, a golden ship across the night sky. The same moon that sailed across the village where Mam slept, Agnes, Rab …

I could not think of them. I looked to my lady, now weaving wraith-like in and out the battlements.

'How long has she walked?' the doctor whispered.

'Since His Majesty went into the field, I think.'

Her voice interrupted me. 'Yet here's a spot.' The queen gazed at her hands, rubbing one against the other.

The doctor fumbled in his pouch. 'I will set down what comes from her to satisfy my remembrance the more strongly.'

'No!' I said, then realised who I spoke to. 'I crave your pardon, gentle sir, but there must be no record.'

He looked at me consideringly.

'Out, damned spot!' The queen's voice rose into an anguished scream. She scrabbled feebly at her nightshift as if she would rip it to shreds. 'Out, I say!'

'What does she speak of?' asked the doctor.

I shook my head dumbly. He must cure her without knowing the cause.

The queen strode along the battlements, her head high, facing an unknown foe. 'One, two. Why, then, 'tis time to do it!' she ordered. 'Hell is murky! Fie, my lord, fie! A soldier, and afeard? What need we fear who knows it, when none can call our power to account?' Her gaze drifted down to her hands again. 'Yet who would have thought the old man to have had so much blood in him,' she whispered.

The doctor stared at her. 'Do you mark that?'

'The Thane of Fife had a wife,' she cried, suddenly alert again. 'Where is she now? What, will these hands never be clean? No more of that, my lord, no more of that. You mar all with this starting!'

The doctor looked at me with sudden understanding. 'We know what we should not,' he said quietly.

Yes. This couldn't be written down. Nor remembered.

'If you could help her,' I whispered. 'Heaven knows what she has known.'

The queen brought her fingers to her face. 'Here's the smell of the blood still,' she mourned. 'All the perfumes of Arabia will not sweeten this little hand.' Her voice rose again to a cry. 'Oh, oh, oh!'

'The heart is sorely charged,' said the doctor.

If only he knew. But I just nodded. 'I would not have such a heart for anything this world has to offer. Will you help her?' I pleaded.

He frowned, watching as my lady prayed in silence again. 'This disease is beyond my practice,' he said abruptly. 'Yet I have known those which have walked in their sleep who have died holily in their beds.'

'Wash your hands,' the queen cried. 'Put on your nightgown; look not so pale. I tell you yet again, Banquo's buried; he cannot come out on his grave.'

'Even so?' muttered the doctor, carefully not looking at me.

I shivered. With each word she proclaimed her guilt. Perhaps I shouldn't have brought the doctor here. But she could not keep roaming each night like this.

'To bed, to bed!' she moaned. 'There's knocking at

the gate. Come, come, come, come. Give me your hand. What's done cannot be undone!'

I ran to her. 'To bed, my lady. Please, to your bed.'

She looked vaguely at me but still didn't see. 'To bed, to bed, to bed,' she muttered again, and stepped back towards the stairs.

'Will she go now to bed?' asked the doctor quietly.

I nodded.

He lowered his voice further still. 'Foul whisperings are abroad: unnatural deeds do breed unnatural troubles. Infected minds to their deaf pillows will discharge their secrets. More needs she the divine than the physician.'

I tried to untangle his speech. 'You mean you can't help her? What about a potion to calm her sleep? There's a yellow flower that blooms in late summer —'

He stared at me, affronted. 'Do you think I am a herb hag, lady? I am a physician. I do not deal in potions.'

'But what *can* you give her?'

He shrugged. 'Pray. May God forgive us all! Look after her, remove from her the means of all annoyance, and still keep eyes upon her.'

In other words, he could offer nothing. He could stitch a wound, or mend a broken bone. He could not heal an anguished mind. Agnes would know what to do, I thought desperately. But I couldn't send for Agnes. It would be a scandal.

'So, good night,' the doctor said firmly. 'She has amazed my sight. I think, but dare not speak.' He bowed stiffly, still annoyed by what he saw as an insult.

I had loosed my lady's secret for nothing, to a man in velvet who held himself too high to use a calming flower.

I slipped down the stairs and opened the queen's door. She slept, tossing uneasily on her pillow, but I didn't think she would walk again. Exhaustion would keep her here the rest of the night.

I needed sleep too. I needed a clear mind too. No clarity here, in a room that smelled of roses and apple wood and power. I climbed the stairs again. I sat upon the battlements, my legs dangling into darkness, and tried to think.

The queen had looked so young up here in her nightshift, without her crown and her scarlet robes. A girl of my age. Yet I'd lived a hundred years more than she, tucked away and tended in her father's castle, then her husband's. What had she known of blood and battle? Only songs and boasts at the dinner table that turned carnage into valour. She had been a child at play, ordering people killed as easily as she might banish a doll she had grown tired of.

And then she saw the blood. She became a queen, who saw the real lives of her people, as she answered their petitions. They were no longer figments to play with. No wonder her mind couldn't hold it all. The blood stained her hands as surely as if she'd thrust the dagger into Duncan herself, into the children who might claim the throne one day, into a mother who might breed more. The guilt she hid by day tore and gnawed at her through the night.

What if I'd done no more than she'd ordered up on the heath, had said nothing about kingship to Macbeth, hadn't promised Banquo his descendants would be kings? Would my lady have been content with Cawdor, and her husband too? No murders and no madness?

If that was so, this was my fault. Each death, each drop of blood, the agony of conscience my lady suffered — all due to me and my pride at manipulating a thane.

How could I undo the wrong I'd so unknowingly begun? Even a queen couldn't give people life again. Nor could evil be withdrawn from the world once it had been done. We could only pray for forgiveness, repent deeply and try to do good instead.

Oh, yes, I repented. But could I do good?

The wind ruffled my hair, bringing the smell of the sea. In daylight, it seemed as though you could see half of Scotland from up here. I could almost smell home — the peat fires, the lanolin of the sheep, the sharp tang of midsummer herbs and heather.

And suddenly the answer came to me. Lady Anne could do little, but Annie Grasseyes had the skills that Agnes had taught her. I could tell a poppy flower from heartsease, and knew how to prepare both, though I'd never done it. Agnes always said powerful poppy must be prepared by the cat, not the kitten. But Agnes wasn't here.

I stood, my mind made up. There was one other I could trust with the queen's secret. Not her ladies, nor Murdoch, but the queen herself. I would seek a private audience with her in the morning and tell her that when she walked on the battlements in nightmares, her feet truly trod the castle's stones. I would tell her I could ease her anguish, calm her mind and body.

Now, in summer, all the flowers I needed would be blooming, and I knew where to find them; which grew in bogs, which in the crevices of courtyard walls. By tonight my lady would have her potion and would walk no more.

And if the queen found peace, maybe Scotland, under Macbeth, might have peace too.

Chapter 17

Midsummer's Eve sat upon the land, the days so fat and fair they squeezed out night till it was only a few hours of shadow before dawn. You could almost hear the grass grow. Larks soared singing above the palace, and lambs wriggled their white tails on the hills.

This morning I would marry Murdoch. This afternoon a messenger would take the tokens to my mother. Tonight I'd be a wife.

I stared at my reflection in the queen's mirror. Her nights had been quiet since I'd made the potion, and the shadows were gone from her eyes in the day. Macbeth strode about the castle like a true king, Lord Murdoch often at his side. I had done my job well, I told myself. A confident king, a queen released from nightmare. I could go to Greymouth with a clear heart.

Why didn't my heart sing?

'Green and gold suit you,' said Lady Margaret, looking as pleased as if the wedding day were her own. She had

169

embroidered much of the gold thread on my gown, and the design was hers too.

The queen laughed. 'Gold suits any woman. Here.' She draped a second long gold chain about my waist, gold flowers matching the gold wheat in my other chain, and Murdoch's jewelled necklace.

Was that reflection me?

'Ma'am, it is too fine.'

'Nonsense.' She touched my cheek gently. 'You are my friend. What you wear today you wear for me.'

I stood silent. Lady Margaret and Lady Ruth were quiet too. A friend. I had never heard the queen use the word before. Perhaps she never had.

'That is more honour than any gold,' I whispered at last.

'I believe that friendship is,' she said quietly. 'My three ladies are a deeper blessing even than my crown.'

She nodded to Lady Margaret and Lady Ruth. 'Your pardon, gentle ladies. I would speak privately with Lady Anne before I lose her.' She smiled lightly. 'To remind her of a wife's duty that you need never bear.'

Lady Margaret returned the smile. I suspected she had never wanted a man in her bed.

Lady Ruth grinned. I suddenly wondered if she might have a life among the servants that we knew nothing of. Or perhaps the queen knew.

The queen waited till the door had shut behind them,

then sat upon the bed and patted the place beside her. 'Sit.'

I obeyed. Despite her words it seemed odd to be sitting side by side. The silence stretched.

'I shall miss you,' she said at last, as simply as any village maid.

'Your Majesty has only to send a message and I will come. You are the queen. You can bid me be with you at any time.'

'Yet one cannot bid friendship.'

'No,' I said. 'But it is there, unbidden. There it will stay too, till we are old and hatching marriages for our grandchildren.'

And it was true, I realised. I hadn't helped her just from duty. This was friendship. Love, perhaps, even if I had not realised it before. The girl who had so unthinkingly promised Macbeth he would be king had more in common than I had realised with the queen she sat with here.

She nodded. 'You know I am with child,' she said abruptly.

'Yes. We guessed it a month ago. Lady Ruth believes you are four months gone.'

She laughed at my honesty. 'What else does Lady Ruth say when I am not present?'

I grinned at her. 'That we must sweeten your pottage with honey else you won't eat it, but not too much or your skin may break out in pimples.'

'Oh dear. I hope she says this only to the two of you?'

'Yes, my lady.' The old term slipped back. 'Just as she tells only us how when you were two years old you hid your chamber pot and the cook found it and served the soup in it and no one but she guessed. We asked how the soup tasted,' I added, 'and she said it was most fine indeed.'

'I am blessed,' she said quietly, 'to have a nurse who loves me, my Lady Margaret to dress me and design the banquet pieces, and to have a friend. It is far more than I deserve. Queens are often not as rich, methinks.'

'I would not know, my lady.'

She gazed out the window, at the purple blaze of heather and the dark green of the forest beyond. 'I repent it all, more deeply than you can ever know. Repent my desperate urgings, repent that night, repent ambition, lust for power, repent what I have made my lord become.'

'I know. You talked and cried of that when you sleepwalked on the battlements,' I said softly.

She stared at me. 'Did I? I ... I thought that was just a dream.'

'Your sleep is quiet now, ma'am.'

'Thanks to your sleeping potion.' She attempted a smile. 'You must send me a gift of it from Greymouth, as I will send you gifts of my affections too, Annie.' It was the first time she had ever used my true name. Had she always realised I was Annie Grasseyes at heart?

'Can good come out of evil?' she whispered. 'If we give Scotland prosperity and peace, shall that be enough?'

I didn't answer. Her Majesty might repent. But the king believed he was invincible and that his house would reign till Birnam Wood should come to Dunsinane. Where would his arrogance, and his sword, go from here?

'I have met two queens,' she continued quietly, as if she knew my thoughts, 'though I was too young to remember much of the first. I do not think their lives were happy.' Her face clouded. 'Nor their deaths.'

I didn't want to blight my wedding day further by asking about the queens' deaths.

It seemed Her Majesty felt the same. She turned to me and took one of my hands in both of hers. 'We must be happy, today of all days! The child I am carrying must be hostage to the kingdom, married for an alliance of state. And the next as well. But if I have a third, perhaps our children may find joy together.'

'I hope my children will serve your family as long as our houses stand,' I said softly.

'And be friends, as we have become.' She stood, and put on her public smile. 'And now your groom will be waiting. Lady Margaret has designed a centrepiece for the feast: a giant loaf that, when broached, shows Paris awarding the golden apple to the Queen of Love.'

I knew from the book I'd read — slowly, to improve my skill — that Paris's prize had led to war. But this was just a loaf of bread. There would be no war now the thanes had all pledged to join the king in battle as soon as he sent word. The English would never lend Malcolm troops when so vast an army could be arranged against them. My worries were foolish. The evil of the pretend charms was all wound up. The harvest would be good, the land at peace.

I glanced at myself in the mirror again. Surely my dress was an omen of my life to come? Green like the grass that would feed the stock; gold like the ears of barley and wheat that would feed the people; flowers to give beauty and happiness.

And the red of my necklace's ruby? I lifted my chin. A sign of riches, a comfortable life and the friendship of a queen.

The chapel was garlanded in white midsummer roses. They'd fade within the hour, but by then I would be married. There was a rustle of silks and velvets and plumed hats as the king and queen entered arm in arm and proceeded down the aisle with me behind them, Lady Ruth and Lady Margaret forming our retinue.

Lord Murdoch waited at the altar. He wore dark blue satin trimmed with velvet, a velvet hat upon his head. Harps played, but I hardly heard them over the beating of my heart. Murdoch glimpsed me behind the king and queen and smiled.

I held my breath as the king and queen raised their hands in an arch to let me through. I stood by Murdoch, drunk on flowers and music, as Their Majesties moved to their robed chairs on either side of the chapel, the queen on my side, the king next to Murdoch.

Murdoch took my hand.

'Sire!'

Muttering took the place of the pleased murmurs behind us as a servant ran up the aisle, heedless of protocol. He kneeled trembling before the king.

Macbeth stood. 'The devil damn thee black, thou cream-faced loon!' he screamed in sudden fury. 'Why do you kneel there trembling like a goose?'

The muttering in the pews grew louder.

So much for a calm king and a peaceful land, I thought. And on my wedding day.

The servant seemed to have hardly enough breath to speak. 'Sire, there are ten thousand —'

'Geese, villain?' demanded the king.

'Soldiers, sire.'

A woman screamed at the back of the chapel. The mutters grew to rumbling.

'Soldiers?' Macbeth shook his head. 'What soldiers, lily-livered boy?'

'The English force, so please you.' The servant bent his head, as if expecting his master's sword to cleave his neck.

Murdoch kissed my hand quickly. 'See to the queen,' he said quietly. 'If that boy speaks the truth, then I must command the guards.' He hesitated, then added, 'God go with you, my lady.'

'And with you, my lord,' I whispered.

Murdoch bowed low to the king. 'Your Majesty.'

Macbeth didn't seem to hear him. Murdoch backed away and out the side door. I ran to the queen.

Macbeth was still raging at the servant. He seemed to have forgotten that the whole court was listening, shifting uneasily, trying to work out if they should run to defend the castle or stay seated here.

'Bring me no more reports. Till Birnam Wood shall come to Dunsinane, there is nothing I need fear. What's the boy Malcolm?' he yelled, staring around as if the servant could produce Duncan's son. 'Was he not born of woman? The spirits that know all told me: "Fear not, Macbeth. No man that's born of woman shall ever have power upon thee."'

I looked up from my curtsey into the queen's face. She gazed at me, her face unreadable.

'Your Majesty?' I whispered. 'I think we should go to your rooms.'

Whether the servant was drunk or crazed, or there really was an army at our walls, I knew I would have no wedding this morning. And the king had just admitted hearing witchcraft.

The queen stood. 'Good friends, I think this ceremony must be postponed,' she said, her voice calm as she formally gave them leave to go. She walked to the chapel door as if moving in a dream, stately in her gold and scarlet robes and her crown, a true queen. We three followed, until she reached the steps and fell. Lady Ruth and I caught her, and half carried her up the stairs and along the corridors.

Below us, men yelled, spilling out of the Great Hall. Spears and shields clanged as they were snatched from the walls. I heard the creaking of the drawbridge being raised. So it was true. An army was at our very gates. I tried to shut my fear away. Murdoch had his duty, and I had mine.

We sat the queen upon her bed.

'Look out the window,' she ordered. Her hands trembled, but her back was straight, her voice was still composed.

I peered out and saw green leaves flash silver in the sunlight. Just a forest. Yet this dawn there had been moorland around the palace, and the bleat of sheep, not trees.

Birnam Wood had come to Dunsinane.

'Well?' demanded the queen.

I caught the silver flash again. Not just leaves, but armour as well. Soldiers, hidden under branches, creeping up and over our defences until they ringed the castle. Even as I watched, the branches parted and I saw cannons and a catapult loaded with a vast boulder.

'My lady ...'

The crash as the boulder hit swamped my words. I peered out again, saw the palace wall crumbled under its force, then withdrew as an arrow whistled past me and buried itself in the queen's bed.

Lady Margaret screamed and backed against the wall.

Lady Ruth moved to the bed and put her arms around the queen as if she were a child again. 'There, there, my lambkin.'

The queen shook her head, a strange smile upon her face. 'No, good nurse, no lambkin now, but a goose for slaughter. There is no help for me; nor you if you are found with me.' She looked at us one by one, her face strangely composed. 'There is a small room off the kitchens, with an even smaller door that can be barred inside. You know it, Lady Margaret. Hide there, the three of you, with food and water. Perhaps the door will hold till order is found once again, and Malcolm might show the mercy his soldiers lose in the lust of battle. Go!'

'I'll not leave you, lambkin,' cried Lady Ruth.

'I am your queen.' And still she looked it, her face calm, her eyes set as hard as any warrior's. 'I know my duty now, and you know yours. If these be my last words to you, then do my bidding. Go!'

I moved towards the door and opened it. If I hadn't, I think they would have stayed, frozen in place. I ran with them, down the first set of stairs, till I saw them join a rush of other women seeking shelter.

I could hear Macbeth bellowing in the hall below. 'Hang out our banners on the outward walls. The cry is still "They come!" Our castle's strength will laugh a siege to scorn.' He held his broadsword high above his head. 'Here let them lie till famine and the ague eat them up. Were they not forced with those that should be ours, we might have met them dareful, beard to beard, and beat them backward home.' He turned. 'What is that noise?'

'It is the cry of women, my good lord,' said someone.

I didn't stay to hear more. I slipped back up the stairs, then along the empty corridor, and opened the door of the queen's chamber.

Chapter 18

My lady kneeled by the bed, her hands raised in prayer. I waited till she had finished, whispering a brief prayer too, for her, for me, for Lady Ruth and Lady Margaret, for Murdoch and for Scotland. Then I helped her up. Her face was calm although her body seemed to have lost its strength.

'How goes my lord?' she asked.

'As a great warrior should be, full of sound and fury.'

'Signifying nothing. He believes that he must win all from those promises we gave him.'

'Surely it is better that he is full of courage now?'

She shrugged. I realised that while I had seen men shattered by battle, she knew more of wars and who might win them.

'Ten thousand soldiers with catapults and battering rams are at our gate,' she said. 'And we have at most four hundred men. No way to get a message to the thanes to call their armies here. Nor time, even if we could. We are lost before we have begun, but my husband does not know it.'

The castle shook again. Another boulder must have crushed more of the palace walls. A roar of triumph rose outside, followed by screams and shouting.

'The enemy has breached the walls,' the queen said quietly. 'I know how this must end. I ordered you to leave me.'

I lifted my chin. 'If Malcolm wins, you are no longer queen but still my friend. I do not leave my friends.'

She almost smiled. 'Then, friend, I need your help. The queen of yesterday will be a plaything for the troops. I will not see it. Can you grant me your sweet potion?'

'My lady ...'

She reached under her pillow and pulled out a dagger. 'Must I use this? Your potion would be kinder.'

I hesitated, then curtseyed one last time, deeply, to the floor. 'I hear Your Majesty and I obey.'

I stepped over to the chest and brought out the flask. Two drops for sleep. Ten drops and you would not wake. I reached for a cup.

'No. Give me all.' She flinched back as another arrow sped through the window, landing on the floor. 'Come swiftly over here.'

I hurried towards her, out of arrow range. She reached for my hand. 'A friend at the last breath, not a servant. I ... I am glad I do not die alone.'

'I will not leave you.'

'Yes,' she said, 'I know.'

She tipped up the flask and drank, her mouth puckering a little at the bitterness. I wondered if she thought of her babe, who would die this morning with her. But better it should die safe with its mother than have its brains bashed out against a wall.

She put down the flask. 'And now I sleep. Sleep that unravels all the threads of care.'

I took her hand again, sitting by her side.

'When they speak of me,' she whispered, 'do not defend my name. Say not "She did it because Duncan was a feeble king", nor "She would have a realm of peace". Let my name live for good, as I did not; a lesson in how ambition can nibble away virtue, till all that is left is death and trickery.'

'My lady, you were so much more than that.'

She smiled. 'I know. But this is what I wish. One good deed to leave this earthly world. Grant me that wish, at least.'

'Ma'am, I will.'

She smiled again. Her eyes closed. I thought she slept, but then she said, 'Promise me you will seek safety?'

'Sleep,' I said softly. I began to sing a lullaby that Mam had sung to me.

'Sleep then my little lamb, sleep,
Soft flows the river so deep ...'

I watched as her breath faded, as her pink cheeks turned to ash. She slept the sleep of death. Even then I kept her hand in mine.

I would not leave her.

Noise rose up, as if a thousand drums beat at our walls. I knew Murdoch would be below, rallying the king's men. I whispered another short prayer for his safety. Loyal Murdoch would not scamper like a puppy from a wolf, but if he survived today he might be captured, ransomed.

Could any person in this castle survive today?

The door crashed open. I thought it would be soldiers. I rose, ready to flee or fight, I knew not which. But the king stood there, his sword dripping with blood. Blood dripped from his arms as well. I looked again and saw it was not his.

He stared at the limp figure on the bed. 'The queen?'

'The queen, my lord, is dead.'

He leaned against the door and shook his head. 'Dead? She should have died hereafter; there would have been a time for such a word.' He shut his eyes, as if the murder of all his hopes was not amidst the screams and yells below. His voice was so soft I could hardly hear it above the clash of armour, the thuds of boulders from the battering rams. 'Tomorrow, and tomorrow, and tomorrow, creeps in this petty pace from day to day to the last syllable of recorded time, and all our yesterdays have lighted fools the way to dusty death.' He opened his eyes and gazed upon his wife. He had loved her once, I thought. Loved her deeply. Did he grieve for her now, or for his hopes? 'Out, out, brief candle!' he muttered, still staring at the figure on the bed.

'My lord,' I said, then stopped. I had no words.

He did. Even in battle, gentlefolk had their words.

He met my eyes for the first time. 'Life's but a walking shadow,' he said, almost conversationally, 'a poor player that struts and frets his hour upon the stage and then is heard no more.' He smiled at me. Or at least I thought the grimace was probably a smile. 'It is a tale told by an idiot, full of sound and fury, signifying nothing.'

'Then why fight if it means nothing?' I demanded, above the tumult, growing closer now. 'Why kill if all here are already doomed?'

But he had lurched upright again and was out the door, his sword raised. I heard his boots pound along the corridor, his voice rising once more in challenge. Birnam Wood had come to Dunsinane but no man of woman born could slay Macbeth. So he believed. And when it was proved wrong — then, as Agnes had said, he would not know.

Shouts turned to screams down in the kitchens. The soldiers must have found the servants. I hoped Lady Margaret and Lady Ruth were locked inside the small chamber, safely guarded by its walls. I hoped Malcolm would show them mercy when at last they must emerge.

I waited, the queen's dagger in my hand. A girl cowering in her lady's chamber.

I would not cower! I was my father's daughter, and Mam's. Mam, whose feet had bled with frostbite as she trapped rabbits in the snow to feed her daughter — till Agnes came and saved us.

Macbeth was wrong. Life mattered. Life and love and friendship. And there *was* life for me. All I must do was fight my way out of the castle towards it.

I gripped the dagger harder and I charged.

Along the corridor, and down the stairs ... and suddenly the battle found me, was all around me — men with swords clashing, jabbing, lurching.

A rough arm knocked me down. Legs. Enemy legs, hairy ones in kilts, ones in leather trousers. I stabbed upward with my dagger, felt it bite into flesh. The flesh moved, carrying my dagger with it. The cut hadn't even slowed him down. What was a girl and a dagger to warriors like these?

The stones were slick with blood. Fresh blood that smelled like tin, was slippery too. A foot stamped on me, and then another. I clutched an ankle and bit hard. Tasted blood and hairy sweat, and then was thrown back, hard.

I rolled into a corner of the room. Looked up. Easy to tell our men from the enemy: the enemy still wore their leaves. The porter lay on the stones, his head cleaved in half. Murdoch clashed swords along the stairs with a man with twigs still poking from his armour. Another thrust and his enemy went down. He turned, saw me, forgot me, and clashed with yet another of the enemy. His life was all the king's now. No part of him was mine.

Words floated down from high above me. Macbeth's voice.

'I will not yield, to kiss the ground before young Malcolm's feet. Though Birnam Wood be come to Dunsinane, being of no woman born, yet I will try the last. Lay on, Macduff, and damned be him that first cries, "Hold, enough!"'

The clamour grew. No shouting now. Men's breaths heaved like their swords. The air was smudged with crimson. Sparks fluttered as blades smashed together. It looked almost like a dance. My wedding dance.

I waited for someone to notice me, for the final blow that would take me from this life. And I deserved it. For my stupid words had led to this. Yet I didn't shut my eyes. Whatever life I had left to live, I would live it.

The sword music changed: a discordant note of hammering underneath the clashes.

I looked towards the outer door and saw Rab McPherson stride into the room, patched with armour from a dozen different suits, a head taller than any man inside the castle, his blacksmith's hammer flashing back and forth.

Almost casually he batted three men away to reach me, yet his hands felt gentle as they hauled me up, balanced me against his armoured side and half dragged me to the door. The air rang with the noise of battle. And still Rab held me as he crossed the drawbridge, ran across bare ground, then found the safety of the forest — the true forest, not the false one carried by Malcolm's men. Out here there was no smell of blood, except on Rab's hammer. A strong stallion, tied to a tree, whinnied at us. He was a warhorse, but wore no armour, only saddlebags.

Rab cleaned his hammer without speaking, both of us still locked in the bloody horror of the castle, then he stripped away his armour and short cloak. Still neither of us had said a word. Actions spoke deeper than words now. Rab hid the armour under a bush. He handed his cloak to me to cover my silk dress and wedding jewels. Suddenly we were simply man and maid.

Voices yelled in triumph.

I looked up at the palace battlements. Macduff stood there, holding up Macbeth's severed head by its hair. Even from here I could make out the king's expression. It almost seemed a smile. Macbeth had peace at last. No more ambition or indecision, or horror at what he'd become.

Rab looked at me, not at the gory trophy. 'Annie, can you walk?'

I found my voice. 'I think so.'

'Ride, if I hold on to you?'

I nodded.

He put his hands about my waist, and lifted me as if I were a feather onto his horse, then swung up behind me. His breath was warm upon my neck. 'Then let's go home,' he said.

The horse ambled across the mountain pass. Slowly I began to understand I was alive, and free, and was myself again. Green shadows and silver light flickered around us. Rab talked to me now, softly, calmly, as he might to a frightened colt: how Malcolm's army had come to Glamis, seeking Macbeth; how Rab kept back their best horse, claiming it was lame, then followed the army to Inverness.

Rab had smoked mutton and stale bannock in the saddlebags that we nibbled as we rode. We drank from streams. Rab put my jewelled necklace and the queen's gold chains in his sporran so we wouldn't tempt thieves, though it would be a careless thief who tried it on with Rab McPherson. He had brought me a dress too, one of Mam's, to put on over my silk dress. He had to cut the seams for me, to make it fit.

'I left your brooch behind,' I said as we skirted a brown loch.

'I'll make another.'

'Rab —'

'No.' His arms tightened about me. 'Whatever you are going to say, I do not need to hear. I am yours, and you are mine. That is enough.'

I found a smile. I didn't know I had one left. 'Yes. That is enough.' Annie Grasseyes and Rab McPherson, as it had always been, if I'd let my ambition fall long enough to see.

'Can you ride all night? There's a moon.'

'I can. But what about the horse?'

'My apprentice, Andrew, is a smith now, halfway along our path. I'll trade horses with him; he'll be glad of this one. Your mam is waiting at my hearth,' he added softly. 'I told her I'd bring you home.'

I nodded, saying nothing. I felt I'd used up most of my life's words in the palace, among folk who were never really mine, in a place that wasn't home.

Chapter 19

Mam waited for me at Rab's house. Her arms around me were even warmer than the fresh bannocks steaming on the hearth. Maggie Two-Teeth was calling me 'mistress' even before Mam had stripped off my bloodied silk dress. I slept that night in Rab's best feather bed, while he slept with the apprentices, Mam's arms about me still. The next day, Sunday, the marriage banns were read at kirk.

Mam and Maggie and I made rabbit stew together, bannocks, leek and rooster soup. We boiled turnips and stirred the porridge pot, while Rab worked with his hammer back in the forge. This was peace, but I didn't deserve it. No one except Mam and Agnes knew what I'd done, and they knew only part of it.

Peace descended on the land too, as suddenly as war. Only the name of our thane changed. Few villagers even cared. No one queried where Rab had been for three days and nights. A blacksmith was too valuable to cross. No one in Malcolm's army would remember the patchwork-armoured giant who'd stormed the palace looking for a girl. No one would care.

When finally the victors rode down to the village, it wasn't to loot or kill, but to visit Big Rab's forge. They had swords and armour that needed mending. Perhaps also they saw the glint in Rab's eye and knew he would defend his own.

Rab and I married quietly. For decency I should have gone back to Agnes's cottage in the weeks before we wed, but Rab bid me and Mam stay, and so we did.

I spent the first week of my marriage in a daze. I didn't deserve this: not Rab and this house; not such safety, nor such happiness. How was I to atone? My lady killed herself, but that was no repentance.

For either a village wife or queen, there is one way only to repent: by doing good. Do your duty, love your husband, and be kind to your neighbours and their children. Every widow would have broth and bannocks from my kitchen, I vowed, for as long as I could bake them. No child would go barefoot in the snow while I could stitch rabbit-skin shoes or jerkins.

Rab buried my gold chains and jewelled necklace. One day, if our village was in need, he'd dig them up — or our sons or grandsons might — and hammer the gold to different forms and sell them.

Sometime during that first year I heard that Lord Murdoch had been captured then ransomed, and was at his father's estate once more. He never came to search for me, nor would I have gone with him if he had done so.

I asked discreetly about Lady Margaret and Lady Ruth from the soldiers who gossiped at Rab's forge, but it seemed no one knew what had happened to them. No one remembers women, in wartime or in peace. In ten years, no one ever looked for me.

The king's witch finder arrived in our village when our firstborn son was nine years old, his twin brothers eight, and my daughter still toddling at my skirts. I'd called her Ingrid, after my lady. No one but me, it seemed, remembered her true name. She had lost it when she married, as women do.

The witch finder rode down from the castle on a horse as small and dark and twisty as himself. Rab stood to meet him in the middle of the road outside the smithy. He had expected him. Men talked while waiting for their horses to be shod.

'Welcome,' Rab said, and gestured to our house, the children standing wide-eyed in the doorway. 'Will you drink a mug of ale? It is my wife's own brewing.'

'Willingly.'

The witch finder dismounted and handed the reins to Tall Tim, one of Rab's apprentices. The witch finder limped as he walked, and was so small he scarcely had to duck under our lintel. A mild-looking man, except for his eyes. They burned.

He settled in the best chair by the fire and I served him the ale and some fresh bannock. I made no castle food these days, not even fruit preserved in honey.

The witch finder gulped his ale, and handed the mug to me to be refilled. 'Ale at the smithy is always welcome. No witch can enter where there's iron. And a smith's ale is always sweet. No witch can enchant a smith's ale and make it sour.'

I stilled. Agnes hadn't crossed our hearth since I was married. But she entered no one's house but her own; it wasn't iron that stopped her. And didn't she wear Rab's iron thistle still on her cloak? Or did she? I rarely saw her now, even though Rab's apprentices still attended to her peat and her thatch, and we sent her meat each time we ate it and oats from our field's harvest.

Fool! I told myself. She'd worn the brooch at my wedding. I was letting this man twist my brain till it was as crooked as his body.

'No witches in this village,' said Rab pleasantly. 'Nor ever have been.'

I smiled at him, my solid husband, so much steadier than I.

The witch finder replied as calmly as if they were discussing fleeces. 'You take good care of this village, Master Smith?'

'I do,' said Rab.

'And you truly believe there has been no witch here?'

'No witch.'

'And yet,' said the witch finder, 'there are rumours of three witches that did meet the usurper king, Macbeth, upon the heath ten years ago and laid an enchantment on him.'

Did this man know I'd served Macbeth's lady? But all in this village had served the thane at some time, large service or small. And surely none would speak of my time at court from loyalty to Rab.

'Three witches,' the witch finder repeated. 'One old, one in good years, one young. And they appeared again, inside a cave near Dunsinane.'

Who had talked? The doctor almost certainly. The actors perhaps, or any of those who'd heard Macbeth boast. Rumours sprang up about the lords and ladies of the court. I'd even heard it said that Macduff, who'd slain Macbeth, was ripped untimely from his mother's womb and so of no woman born. A man's story that. Every child is born of a woman's body, even when the mother does not live.

'Then Dunsinane is where you must search for them,' said Rab firmly. 'There are no witches in my village, sir.'

'Then you will not object to my questioning the people?'

A heartbeat's hesitation. 'No.'

And so he did, most gently, house to house, sipping their ale and eating their bannocks. And that Sunday at the kirk, he stood up and faced the congregation.

'All unknowing,' he said sternly, 'a witch has been harboured here. Her name is Agnes.'

My breath stabbed me. I could not move.

Rab stood. 'Agnes is no witch, sir. A harmless woman, good with herbs.' He looked around. 'Is that not so?'

The people muttered agreement, but none too loud. Why did they not yell at the witch finder in protest? Agnes had helped them all.

Then I understood. They were scared, as I was scared. *Keep your head down*, Agnes had warned me. And now we were all doing it.

'And yet Agnes does not come to kirk today?' the witch finder asked Rab, still with that steady smile.

'That is her way, sir. She does come sometimes.'

'Her way indeed.' The witch finder fixed him with his dark eyes. 'We shall see when she is put to the fire if she confesses what she is and the names of her accomplices.'

Men from the castle came to pile wood upon the green outside the smithy. No village man would do it, but nor did they fight the soldiers to stop them. Green wood at the base, then dryer, but not too dry so the flames wouldn't consume her before she talked. He knew his job, the witch finder.

Rab argued with the witch finder all that week, and others of the village too. Not many. Not enough. But some.

I said nothing.

The witch finder must have known that Mam and I had shared Agnes's cottage all those years. Mam had died of congestion of the lungs two years before, and no broths of mine nor Agnes's goose fat could save her. And I lived with the smith now, with iron all about. I couldn't be a witch, nor could Mam — unless Agnes said we were. What would happen to my children and Rab if I was labelled as a witch and burned? Would they be burned too?

The soldiers dragged Agnes, bound, to the stake. She'd grown so bent in the last years, they couldn't tie her higher than her waist.

She didn't look at them or the stake.

She looked at me. She even smiled, a tiny smile, just for a second. A smile to me.

A soldier handed the witch finder a flaming torch. He held it above his head.

'Will you confess?' he asked Agnes, his voice still gentle, almost as you'd ask a child.

Agnes looked at him in contempt. She said nothing.

'If you confess, you will be strangled. It is an easier death than flames.'

Agnes gazed at my children. That small smile flashed again. She nodded to herself, then looked down at her feet.

A baby sobbed, not for Agnes but because its ma didn't give it suck. No one in the whole crowd cried for Agnes, for all she'd helped each one of them with herbs and potions. Were they afraid of what an old woman might mumble in her agony?

I wasn't afraid. Those smiles had told me Agnes wouldn't speak.

'One last chance,' said the witch finder, his voice harder now.

Agnes grinned at him, showing her white teeth, and spat.

The witch finder bent and touched torch to wood. It flared so fast it must have been laced with fat. But after that, the flames only snickered, not even belching smoke, so Agnes was conscious as her skirt caught fire.

She stared straight ahead as her legs blistered and began to char, as the flames crept up her body.

'Talk!' shouted the witch finder, his eyes blazing fiercer than the flames. 'Give us names. You may be strangled yet!'

Agnes screamed.

Rab lifted two stones. He pitched the first, his blacksmith's hands strong and true. The stone landed on Agnes's forehead, but not quite hard enough to knock her out. Two soldiers suddenly had Rab's arms. It took six more to hold him down.

Still Agnes screamed. The sun rose high, and higher still. Two hours perhaps, as castle folk might reckon it. Two hours to die.

And then silence, except for the snickering of the flames. What was left didn't seem to ever have been a woman. The crowd crept away, ashamed perhaps that they hadn't thrown stones too. Glad Agnes had said no names; worried that maybe a neighbour knew they'd once gone to her cottage for a love charm or a potion.

Maggie Two-Teeth ushered our children home. And still I stood there. It began to rain.

'Annie,' said Rab.

I turned to him and rested my head on his chest. When I lifted it at last, I found the witch finder observing us.

'You were good friends with the witch,' he said to me.

'She was no witch.' How was it now, too late, that I found my courage? 'An old woman skilled with herbs who let people think they worked better than they did. She sheltered my mam and me for years after my father died.'

'You were good friends,' he repeated.

'No, Agnes wasn't a friend.' I saw he knew it for the truth, could read it in my face. 'I had a friend once, but long ago. She died. But I'm grateful for the care Agnes gave my mam and me. She was good to me. Agnes was good to all of us. Everyone in this village owes her gratitude, and everyone at the castle too, for her goose-fat liniment and Old Man's Bottom.'

He frowned. 'Old Man's Bottom?'

'A herb,' I said wearily. 'Good for aching joints. So Agnes said.'

'She told you nothing else? Nothing of witchcraft?'

'No,' I said. 'Nothing of that. Ever.'

Once more he heard the truth.

'Your mother lived within the smithy until her death?' he asked.

'She did,' said Rab. 'And never scared of iron neither.'

Except swords, I thought. Mam didn't like it when Rab mended or forged them. But I didn't say that now for this twisted man to corrupt.

He left, at last. And Rab buried Agnes's ashes, outside the graveyard. It was better, the minister decided. I hadn't the will to argue. Besides, likely Agnes would have preferred the hillside.

And so I lived, and still live now. I sing in the kirk each Sunday, with Rab and our children and grandchildren by my side. I visit the poor and the sick with bannocks and pots of soup. I am accounted a good woman. I try hard to be good.

I am not a witch, nor could ever be; nor have I ever met one. There was no magic, ever, just play-acting and ambition. If Agnes had been a witch, she could have spirited herself away, not stood there screaming as her face melted and flared.

Only then, in that last second, did she meet my eyes. She'd saved me, her glance told me. Because if she had vanished, not by magic but under a dark cloak on a dark night, as soon as the witch finder arrived, there'd have been whispers to the witch finder about Mam and me.

So an old woman burned and I stood safe. That's what I think sometimes, when the memory wakes me before the rooster crows and Rab lies snoring and warm beside me.

Other times, I wonder if evil creeps about the world, worming into people's lives without them knowing its true face. And then day's light seeps across the world and the hens cackle, and I know that love matters most, and true evil is impossible again.

Or is it? I do not know. But this I know for sure.

My lady died because of words I said, unthinking, arrogant, on the heath.

And even as Agnes screamed at the stake, her body on fire, I could not call to her and say, 'I'm sorry.'

For all of it. I didn't mean to do it.

I'm sorry.

Author's Notes

Once upon a time in Brisbane, a schoolgirl was given the role of Third Witch in a semi-professional production of *Macbeth*. 'Semi-professional' was common in the 1960s; it meant the director and main actors were paid, but those with minor roles were not.

It was magnificent: the rolling words; the dry ice creating a mist across the stage; the clash of genuine broadswords that gave off sparks, and were so heavy that after the evening performance on the Saturday, when we'd also played a matinée, Macbeth collapsed after the battle and had to be supported at the curtain call. Two wolfhounds accompanied Lady Macbeth everywhere she went, royally holding up their heads and obeying without signals as they were her own dogs.

The play was carried by the main actors and the superb director. The rest of us were okay. Enough so that the audience sat still for twenty seconds before they stood to applaud — that silence an actor longs for even more than the cheers, showing how lost people were within the play.

My richest memory is sitting on a pile of scenery in costume, hunchbacked and many-warted, studying for my economics exam the next morning, while Banquo, in rich velvets, explained Marxist economics to me. (I only wanted to know how to calculate Gross National Product.) How many times did we rehearse? I didn't count. I do remember the director's and actors' shock when I turned up in my school uniform and they realised how old — or young — I was. At each rehearsal I drank in the words, and have kept them with me all my life, the power and the music.

Years later, when I researched the true history of Macbeth, I discovered that Shakespeare had changed history and made him a villain, his wife a mad murderess, and added Banquo to a story where he'd never been in history. The real Macbeth was a great and good man, elected leader by the heads of the clans and the bishops, a devout Christian; and his wife had opened schools and orphanages, and managed the country while her husband went on pilgrimage to Rome. Shakespeare slandered them deliberately to please his new patron and ruler, King James I.

During the reign of Elizabeth I, Shakespeare was able to write women of fire and courage. But James I wasn't fond of women, and he deeply disliked and distrusted women rulers, such as the mother he never knew who was executed as a traitor. King James wrote a book about how to identify witches and slaughter them, and Banquo was his ancestor, which is why he ended up in Shakespeare's play.

Macbeth was one of Shakespeare's last plays, the work of a mature writer who knew his craft and his audience. It is his best, I think, in terms of putting the folly of ambition and deep disillusionment into the mouths of others. I love the play. But I feel deeply guilty about writing another book that slanders a good and great man and his strong and generous wife.

There is nothing in my book that contradicts the play, though it does put new interpretations on parts of it. Nor do I think Shakespeare would have minded a book based on his work. (If I did, I'd never have begun this series.) I hope he would take my adaptation as the homage it is intended to be.

Shakespeare based his own plays on others' work, and speeches were changed from performance to performance depending on the audience. He'd add more blood if playing in a tavern during the plague years when London's theatres were shut; or mime if the company went abroad and didn't know the language; and probably longer, more complex speeches when playing before that woman of extraordinary intelligence, many languages and enormous education, Queen Elizabeth I.

Third Witch is not set in the time of the real Macbeth — that much loved excellent ruler with his deeply competent and compassionate wife — but in an imaginary world more like Shakespeare's England, where his play is set. The play is imaginary too, not history. As in Shakespeare's original work, no character in this book resembles any person, alive or dead, and certainly not from history.

THE THREE WITCHES

Why were the three witches on the heath waiting for Macbeth?

For King James I and Shakespeare, innate evil might have been reason enough, with Lady Macbeth's ambition encouraging further evil. But I don't believe in innate evil. When evil is done, there is a reason for it. And so in this book there is a reason for the witches to be up on the heath and in the cave; and in neither case is it to practise witchcraft.

The witches in *Macbeth* were part of the mad illusion of King James I, an absolute monarch who forced his insanity across his kingdom. His fantasies that witches threatened his kingdom encompassed not only those who followed ancient religions, but anyone who was a convenient scapegoat if a cow's milk dried up, or plague killed a village, or someone had a daughter instead of a son. James I even believed that witchcraft had caused the storms that had delayed his ship leaving Denmark.

AGNES'S DEATH

The true sin in this book isn't the Macbeths' plotting, even murdering their king. War and killing were games played by the kings and lords and gentlemen in this book. King Duncan's wars had killed many, many people. At last the murder games he played led to his death.

But Annie betrayed Agnes with her arrogance, thinking that because she lived with lords and ladies, she didn't need to listen to the warnings of a village wisewoman. Because of that, Agnes died. But even in her agony, Agnes stayed loyal to Annie and to the villagers who owed her so much. It would have been easy for Agnes to melt into the darkness before the witch finder arrived; easy to yell out names to accuse others so as to escape the pain at the stake.

Agnes kept her integrity.

Kings led their helpless people off to war, and did not care how many died or were left crippled. Even if Agnes would not use the word 'love', that is what she gave her people.

There were few good roads in Shakespeare's time, and even fewer suitable for coaches. People walked, or rode, or were carried in chairs or litters.

SOME RECIPES

Liniment for aching bones

WARNING: Do not use this on broken skin. Try a tiny bit on the inside of your wrist first, in case you're allergic to any of the ingredients. Do not use the liniment again if your skin turns red.

Ingredients

    6 tablespoons of beeswax (try a beeswax candle)

    6 tablespoons of almond oil

    6 drops of ginger oil

    10 drops of peppermint oil

    6 drops of lavender oil

    (You can use the herbs themselves, but that is a longer and more complicated process.)

Method

In a saucepan on a very low heat, melt the beeswax in the almond oil.

Turn off the heat and leave to cool for a minute, then add the ginger, peppermint and lavender oils.

Immediately pour the mixture into a small wide-mouthed jar that's sitting on a wooden surface (so it doesn't crack), and seal at once.

Keep in a cool dark place and apply as necessary. The liniment should last at least a year.

Herbed flap of mutton
Ask your butcher to prepare a mutton flap for you.

Ingredients
  1 cup of fresh breadcrumbs
  Juice of 1 lemon or 1 sour orange
  1 tablespoon of fresh thyme leaves (no stems)
  6 sage leaves, torn
  6 onions, peeled and chopped
  6 cloves of garlic, chopped (in the castle, they'd have used the tops of the wild garlic that still grows in Scotland)
  3 tablespoons of melted butter
  1 mutton flap

Method
Mix together all the stuffing ingredients. Spread out the mutton flap. Scatter the stuffing over it.

Roll up the flap and tie it securely with kitchen string.

Place the rolled flap in an oven dish and bake at 160°C for three hours, so the fat melts away and leaves the meat tender.

Cut away the string before you serve it. The roll should keep its shape.

Slice it thinly and eat it with gravy or redcurrant jelly. It is also delicious cold.

Bannocks
Bannocks used to be baked on the hot hearthstones in front of the fire, not in an oven. There were probably as many recipes as there were Scottish cooks. This is a good one.

Ingredients
- 1 cup of rolled oats, whizzed in the blender till they look like flour
- 1 cup of self-raising flour (barley flour was also used)
- 6 tablespoons of butter, or any solid fat (don't worry if the measurement isn't exact, as it's hard to get an exact spoonful of butter)
- ⅓ of a cup of buttermilk, or a little more
- Extra butter

Method
Combine the oats and flour.

Rub the butter into the oat and flour mixture to get a texture like breadcrumbs.

Add the buttermilk and stir gently. If the mixture is too dry, add a little more buttermilk.

Put a frying pan on a low heat.

Gently form the mixture into a round, then flatten it so it's like a thick pancake and will fit in the pan.

Melt the extra butter in the pan.

As soon as the butter has melted, lay the bannock in the pan. Fry gently until the crust is pale brown. (Lift the edge carefully with a spatula or egg slice to see.)

Turn the bannock over with the spatula or egg slice, again carefully as it will be brittle. Fry until the base is pale brown. By now it will have risen to twice its original size.

Break off a bit to check it's cooked all the way through. If it is, serve with more butter, or with slices of cheese or ricotta mixed with chopped chives. Ricotta is similar to the fresh 'green cheese' made in the time of the book.

It's certainly not traditional, but I like it with chilli jam, as well as cheese.

And yes, it can be baked in the oven too. It's best fresh, but lasts a day or two in a sealed container, and can be reheated.

Optional: Scatter rock salt on either side of the bannock before placing it in the pan.

To make sweet bannock: Add 6 tablespoons of caster sugar and/or a cup of dried currants or blueberries.

Acknowledgements

As always, fair acknowledgement would be longer than this book. But to Lisa, Cristina, Nicola and Kate, thank you for both this series and the breadth of your help with it. Angela, as always, has turned mess into text. Bryan has tolerated long lectures on Shakespeare's motivations while expertly pretending to listen while reading *New Scientist*.

Thank you to my friends from St Bede's, and Virginia too, for reminding me in so many ways, at so many times, that true evil does not exist, but just the ignorance or twisted anguish that creates tragedy instead of love.

And to the long-ago producer who (unknowingly) gave a fifteen-year-old girl a part in the Scottish play — thank you. You changed my life in many ways, including hearing the beauty of words day on day and week on week, at a time in my life when I most needed them.

Finally, of course, to WS, 'the only begetter of these words', thank you, a million times, and thank you again.

Jackie French AM is an award-winning writer, wombat negotiator, the 2014–2015 Australian Children's Laureate and the 2015 Senior Australian of the Year. She is regarded as one of Australia's most popular children's authors and writes across all genres — from picture books, history, fantasy, ecology and sci-fi to her much loved historical fiction. 'Share a Story' was the primary philosophy behind Jackie's two-year term as Laureate.

jackiefrench.com
facebook.com/authorjackiefrench

Titles by Jackie French

Australian Historical

Somewhere Around the Corner • Dancing with Ben Hall
Daughter of the Regiment • Soldier on the Hill • Valley of Gold
Tom Appleby, Convict Boy • A Rose for the Anzac Boys
The Night They Stormed Eureka • Nanberry: Black Brother White
Pennies for Hitler

General Historical

Hitler's Daughter • Lady Dance • How the Finnegans Saved the Ship
The White Ship • They Came on Viking Ships • Macbeth and Son
Pharaoh • Oracle • I am Juliet • Ophelia: Queen of Denmark
The Diary of William Shakespeare, Gentleman
Goodbye, Mr Hitler • Third Witch

Fiction

Rain Stones • Walking the Boundaries • The Secret Beach
Summerland • A Wombat Named Bosco • Beyond the Boundaries
The Warrior: The Story of a Wombat
The Book of Unicorns • Tajore Arkle
Missing You, Love Sara • Dark Wind Blowing
Ride the Wild Wind: The Golden Pony and Other Stories
Refuge • The Book of Horses and Unicorns

Non-Fiction

A Year in the Valley • How the Aliens from Alpha Centauri
Invaded My Maths Class and Turned Me into a Writer
How to Guzzle Your Garden • The Book of Challenges
The Fascinating History of Your Lunch
To the Moon and Back • The Secret World of Wombats
How High Can a Kangaroo Hop?
Let the Land Speak: How the Land Created Our Nation
I Spy a Great Reader

The Animal Stars Series

The Goat Who Sailed the World • The Dog Who Loved a Queen
The Camel Who Crossed Australia
The Donkey Who Carried the Wounded
The Horse Who Bit a Bushranger
Dingo: The Dog Who Conquered a Continent

The Matilda Saga

1. A Waltz for Matilda • 2. The Girl from Snowy River
3. The Road to Gundagai • 4. To Love a Sunburnt Country
5. The Ghost by the Billabong • 6. If Blood Should Stain the Wattle